To Gene
To Deborah Morgan

MURIEL CANFIELD KANOZA was born in Oak Park, Illinois, and raised in suburban Chicago. She married in 1956 and has three children. She and her husband became Christians after 17 years of marriage. She has been a full-time writer for the past five years. She has a degree in English Education from Miami University. This is Muriel's second book. The first was *I Wish I Could Say I Love You*, Bethany House Publishers, 1983.

1

*P*erhaps it was the way the mist wreathed the tower of The Hamlet Inn that made Anne Lindsey shudder. Or maybe it was the way the pines swept the moon like witches' brooms. Or was she having a premonition? *People sometimes do*, she thought. *Sometimes they sense an accident or fire or something awful about to happen—and then it does happen.*

Stop it! Anne chided herself. *You don't even believe in witches' brooms. This is a gloomy place and you're just letting your imagination run wild.* Immediately, the tower took on a cleaner line and the pines became ordinary. She was again filled with the excitement she had held the entire bus trip from Reily.

Despite her heavy suitcase, she hurried across the boardwalk, up the steps to the veranda that wrapped the front and sides of the inn, and through the shadows of gingerbread that latticed the flooring. As she stepped into the lobby, her excitement reached such heights that she expected to run head-on into Mark McGill, the son of the inn's owners.

She didn't.

But she had pictured him so many times this last year that she saw him clearly in her mind. He was a little taller than her father, who was exactly six feet, and he had a thick head of black hair that she would love to touch; though, of course, she never had. His eyes were the hard blue of an

August sky, and contrasted strikingly with his black hair. His chin was angular and strong. Perhaps it would have been too strongly defined if it weren't for the hint of a dimple softening it. His mouth was wide, and he had a slow smile, which he fully controlled.

That was Mark: in control. Though he was only 26, he already had his own law practice in downtown Reily. He was brilliant, and Anne was totally enamored with him. He may not have felt the same about her, but this year, if all went as she hoped, he would. She had worked at The Hamlet Inn the last two summers as a waitress and had signed on again this year with the express hope of catching his attention. As she considered the prospect, she felt confident and held her small frame erect. She was almost sure he'd notice her. After all, she was nineteen and he'd see that she wasn't a child anymore!

Anne hurried to the front desk. Facing her was Mark's sister Emma, her face stern and unsmiling in the light of the hurricane lamps behind her. As could be expected, Emma was anything but warm and didn't come around the counter to welcome her.

"Hi, Miss McGill," Anne said, automatically using the formal title Emma required of the staff.

For two years Anne had struggled to like Emma. Anne was discouraged because she hadn't yet succeeded but was determined to try harder this year. The task, however, would be formidable. Emma was thirty-five, an unmarried, plain-looking women with a boxy frame and a voice as sour as green apples. She had one good point, and that was her glorious auburn hair. Unfortunately, she always coiled it into a stiff bun.

Emma, along with her mother Tessie, her father Jim, her brother Kevin, and her uncle (nicknamed Little Uncle) operated The Hamlet Inn. Emma, having the best business mind of the family, managed the front desk. Though Mark didn't work at the inn, he lived there.

Anne wondered if she should ask if Mark was there, then decided against it. Emma would somehow misinterpret the question, perhaps even tell Mark she was looking for him. Mark in turn might think she was chasing him. . . .

Because Emma abhorred tardiness, she barked out the expected comment: "You're over two hours late, Anne. You were expected at eight."

Anne set down her suitcase and braced herself for another difficult tirade. "I—I'm sorry. I had some trouble. Dad's car broke down and I had to take the bus."

"That shouldn't have prevented you from phoning in the delay."

"But I tried three times—your line was busy."

"You could have kept trying."

"I couldn't. I was using the garage phone and didn't want to tie up their line any longer."

"Humph," Emma conceded, jabbing a strand of hair back into her bun with a pencil. She handed Anne a key. "You won't be where you were last summer. You'll be in room three-thirty-four, the room opposite the tower stairs."

"Is my roommate here?" The McGills had hired two summer waitresses, Anne and the girl who would room with her. Part-time help from Reily would relieve Anne and her roommate on their days off.

"Yes," Emma answered curtly.

"Is she from around here?"

"No."

Emma hated to be questioned, but curiosity kept Anne probing. "Where is she from, then?"

"Chicago."

"Does she go to school?"

Emma's exasperation began to show. "*Yes.* Northwestern University."

"What year is she in?"

"Sophomore."

"Will she—"

Emma was adamant now. "I suggest you direct any further questions to her." She then dismissed Anne with, "I'd say she's expecting you—*now*."

Anne picked up her suitcase. "I'll see you in the morning."

"See that you're in the dining room at six-thirty," Emma muttered.

Anne left, reaffirming her resolve to like Emma, no matter how difficult she was. Though the suitcase was heavy, she decided against taking the elevator, which in its arthritic state reluctantly granted each upward inch. She didn't have the patience to wait.

Besides that, there was a chance she might meet Mark on the stairs. Excitement rose within her, then dimmed as she remembered that her father wouldn't be pleased if he knew she had an interest in Mark. But she couldn't think about that, at least not now. Things would work out in due time.

2

Oh, no! Anne thought as she stepped into the third-floor corridor. Her disappointment in not meeting Mark was overcome by the surprise before her. Tessie McGill was the family decorator, and over the winter her feeble grasp of appropriate decor had slipped completely. The doorknobs had been painted canary yellow, the doorjambs emerald green, and the doors had been varnished like mirrors. In wild accompaniment the hallway had been papered in an orange, green, and yellow stripe.

Tessie must be making an all-out attempt to attract guests, Anne thought. *But won't the crazy color scheme drive the guests away!* She earnestly hoped not.

One hundred years ago the 102-room inn had been one of the more elegant resorts in Michigan and was often booked to capacity. But it had long since faded and fallen into disrepair, and the McGills struggled to keep it half full. The inn lacked sufficient proceeds to support the McGills; therefore during the winter, when the inn was closed to guests, the McGills operated Hamlet Inn Exquisite Foods, a catering service known throughout the county for its fine food.

When Anne came to 334, she knocked before entering so as not to startle her roommate. "Come on in," came the muffled reply.

Her roommate was sitting on the edge of her bed, bent over like a paper clip, brushing a mass of black hair that

11

touched her ankles. When she raised her head the waves rippled around her gorgeous face. Her cheekbones were high and her eyes were a striking sea green. "I'm Madeline Radcliff," she said in a cultivated voice.

Anne held back her surprise and introduced herself, while Madeline pulled a package of cigarettes as long as her hand from the nightstand. "Where are you from?" Madeline asked.

"Oh, I'm from Reily." Though Reily was just nine miles north, Anne had decided to save the time driving back and forth. Also, of course, the more time she spent here, the more chances there would be to see Mark.

"This place is a wreck," Madeline said with disgust, waving her cigarette at a dresser. "Look at that thing. The mirror's cracked and the bottom drawer's seething with bugs. I hope you don't mind, but I left it for you—I hate bugs."

"What kind of bugs?" Anne said squeamishly.

Madeline shrugged. "I don't know—some kind of crispy, brown things."

Prepared to jump from the swarm, Anne gingerly opened the bottom drawer. Her eyes widened in surprise as she saw two dead beetles on their backs.

Without noting Anne's reaction, Madeline continued her complaint. "For two cents I'd leave this place. I wouldn't even be here if my modeling job at Berkshire's hadn't fallen through."

"Berkshire's?"

Madeline's eyes widened. "You don't know Berkshire's?"

"Well, no."

"It's in Chicago. They stock nothing but the best in designer clothing."

Anne noted that the one small closet was nearly filled with Madeline's clothes. And if the outfit Madeline had on was representative of the rest of her things, they were all from stores like Berkshire's. She wore a beautifully cut, straight-line black skirt, a white silk blouse, and stunning three-inch heels.

Anne lifted her suitcase to her bed and started to unpack her jeans, shorts, and skirts. Her clothes seemed appropriate for a place like The Hamlet Inn. Madeline's didn't. In fact, Madeline didn't seem to belong here. It was as if she had wandered in by mistake.

Anne squeezed her skirts and dresses into the closet, then stacked her jeans and shorts on the dresser. Seemingly unaware that Anne was inconvenienced, Madeline lit another cigarette, blew the smoke out in a practiced line, and explained that she was studying drama at Northwestern. She intended to become a famous actress—not one of those tacky types that were all looks and no talent, but an accomplished actress in the classical sense. She would do only quality scripts. She would definitely *not* prostitute her talent. Madeline then turned to Anne, "So, what about you? What do you do?"

Next to Madeline's pursuits, Anne's seemed quite dull. "I go to Bible school in Reily," she replied almost apologetically.

Anne had just completed the first of a four-year missionary training program. The school had one hundred students, some taking courses to prepare for vocations within the local church, some studying for the mission field. Though the school was a mile from her home, Anne lived in a dormitory with forty girls, believing the experience would broaden and mature her. Anne's father, the Reverend Dr. John Lindsey, pastored a large church in Reily, and Anne hoped to be one of its missionaries when she graduated. Sometimes, though, she wondered if she would carry through with her plan. Her mother had died seven years ago in an automobile accident, leaving Anne and her father alone. They had become quite close. She often wondered if she could bear to be thousands of miles from him. And what if Mark came to love her? She couldn't possibly leave Reily!

Madeline's eyebrows arched in utter amazement. "*Bible school!* For what?"

"To be a missionary."

Madeline was dumbfounded. "A missionary! You'll be swallowed up in poverty! I'd forget it if I were you. I don't say that because I don't believe in God and heaven and all that, which I don't—I say it because you've got to be practical."

"This isn't the kind of thing a person can be practical about."

"A person can be practical about anything," Madeline said and changed the subject. "What do you do for fun around here?"

"Swim, fish, climb the sand dunes. Sometimes—"

"I mean *fun.* I mean men, honey, *men!*"

Anne laughed at Madeline's intensity, then said, "There are usually lots around. There are the guests, and there's some male help." *And there's Mark,* Anne thought, not mentioning his name.

"Then maybe this place'll be all right." Madeline poked her cigarette in Anne's direction. "Hurry up and finish unpacking and take me on a tour."

Anne finished quickly, hoping that on the tour she would run into Mark. She went to the mirror, ran a comb through her blond hair, and freshened her lipstick. As a last touch, she powdered the sprinkle of freckles on her nose. When she was at home, she had felt she looked her best, but now she wondered. She was several inches shorter than Madeline; maybe she was too short. Her friends said she had a country-fresh beauty, a fact which she had never thought much about until now. *Am I really pretty?* she wondered.

Anne caught Madeline's reflection in the mirror. Suddenly she dwindled under the impact of Madeline's beauty, her expensive clothes and makeup—her seeming ability to shine like the lights of Chicago. *If only I looked like her, Mark would surely notice me,* Anne thought.

Stop this! Anne chided herself. *If he doesn't like me as I am, then I don't want him. But he WILL notice me, won't he?*

3

$\mathcal{M}$ark wasn't in the kitchen, nor in the game room, where Madeline ran her finger along the edge of a pool table, remarking that pool was a "low-class" activity. Her father was a wealthy investor and her parents belonged to an exclusive country club. Tennis and golf were more her games.

Nor was Mark in the dining room, where Madeline dropped her sophisticated preferences and said she found the pine walls and bentwood chairs cozy. In a wistful tone she explained that her parents' apartment in a Chicago high-rise made her nervous. "It's all concrete. It's even got concrete floors," she said—"though, of course, Dad had them covered with the best carpeting." A hurt expression crossed Madeline's face. "But I don't want to talk about him. Where to next?"

"To the beach," Anne said eagerly. Sometimes at night Mark walked along the shore of Lake Crystal, which fronted the inn. Nobody knew why the lake was called Lake Crystal, for it was anything but crystal clear. But the lake did have good beaches and was well known for its gamy largemouth and smallmouth bass.

The inn was on a bluff and Anne led Madeline to the steep flight of stairs that descended to the lake. "You'd better take off your heels," Anne said. "You could kill yourself."

"But I don't want to wreck my stockings." To Anne's surprise Madeline sailed down without touching the rail.

At the base of the steps a pier lined with benches and

comma-shaped pole lamps ran about a hundred feet into Lake Crystal. To the left of the pier was a long, narrow boathouse. Beyond the boathouse was the beach.

Before she saw his features clearly, Anne recognized his irregular gait, the result of a fractured knee in a college football game. Mark was walking along the path in front of the boathouse. The air around her became light, more poignant as she marked each step he took toward her. When he reached the midpoint of the boathouse, Anne clearly saw his handsome, angular face, his wavy hair that dipped boyishly over his forehead, making him look somewhat vulnerable.

Madeline became aware of him then. "*Wow*, who's he?" she gasped.

"Mark McGill, one of the owners' sons." Anne didn't take her eyes off him.

"He's so handsome."

"Yes." Anne continued to watch him.

He adjusted a telescope he had tucked under his arm; then seeing Anne, he quickened his stride and called, "Hey, Anne."

Anne's knees weakened.

A few more steps and he was in front of her, gathering her in his strong arms. For a moment she was uncomfortable, overwhelmed by the unexpected gesture and the sense of her heart beating in her throat.

It's just a brotherly hug, she thought wildly. *Don't make more of it than it is.*

He grasped her shoulders and held her out from him, studying her as he might a child. "You've grown," he said.

Her head was light, but not so light that she couldn't respond. "I'm not a child! I haven't grown an inch in three years."

He laughed and ruffled her hair, ignoring her retort.

Anne's hopes were dashed. He had actually refused to notice that she was a *woman*. Well, someday he *would* notice.

She would find a way to make sure he did! Anne then introduced Madeline to Mark, casually adding, "She's the other waitress."

"Temporarily, that is," Madeline amended, explaining her plans to become a quality actress.

"Really?" he said with interest.

"Yes—I've got my life laid out."

"I believe in setting goals too."

"Oh—what are yours?"

"To be a successful attorney."

"So you're an attorney!" Madeline said in an impressed tone. "Frankly, waitress work is a bit beneath me . . . but actually it could be valuable."

"How's that?" said Mark.

"If I'm called upon to play the part of a waitress or similar profession, I'll be able to do so accurately."

Mark gave Madeline that lazy grin of his and Anne became instantly jealous. He should be smiling at her! She blurted, "You could never work all the jobs of all the characters you'll be portraying."

"Of course not, Anne. I'm simply saying there's value in waiting on tables."

"You're right," said Mark. "I like your positive approach."

Madeline isn't a bit positive, Anne thought. She was putting on a front. If only Mark knew that Madeline considered the inn a dump.

Together they turned toward the stairs. An old couple, each as stout as the other, thumped uncertainly down. They clutched each other with one hand and the oak-limb banister with the other.

Fearing they would topple, Anne took a step toward them. Mark stopped her. "They'll be all right," he whispered. "Mom says they make it safely down every night."

Anne kept an eye on the pair until they reached the pier;

then her attention turned to Madeline again. She was thinking that Madeline was the most irritating, vain person she had ever known.

Madeline touched Mark's telescope and gazed into his eyes. "How interesting that you study the stars. I've always wondered how to tell a star from a planet."

"Stars twinkle, planets don't."

"Of course, I'd forgotten." She laughed whimsicaly at her lapse of memory.

Mark laughed too, and they headed for the end of the pier, where he could best show her the difference between a star and a planet. "So you won't forget," he said.

Anne followed. Were these the first steps in a long summer of trailing after them? They couldn't be. Mark couldn't be interested in Madeline. He had only known her for twenty minutes!

But he *was* interested. By the time they reached the end of the pier, he had asked her to climb the dunes when she finished working breakfast. "You too," he said to Anne offhandedly.

The invitation was an afterthought, which Anne couldn't bear. Well, she wouldn't tag along after them. She'd die first. "I won't be able to," she said.

"Why?" he asked.

Her lips trembled. She knew the sign; she was about to cry. She had to get out of there *now*. Her words ran together and she was moving away almost before she finished saying, "Oh, I'm busy tomorrow—good-night."

Anne began to run, tears flowing down her face as her feet pounded against the shaky boards of the pier.

This had turned out to be a horrible evening!

She couldn't stand Madeline.

Anne's jealousy grew, and by the time she threw open her door, she felt as if she would choke on it. She ran to the window and gripped the sill until her knuckles turned white. *Go home, Madeline!* she thought. *Please go home!*

4

*P*ack *up your gigantic trunk and go back to Chicago!*
Anne thought, glaring at Madeline's trunk in the corner,
then peering down through the pines toward several lamp-
posts, any one of which Madeline and Mark might be standing under.

I'll handle the dining room by myself, she silently declared.

In an attempt to dissipate her anger, Anne went to the
dresser and drove her brush through her hair, hardly noticing that the bristles scratched her neck.

When Madeline came in a few minutes later, she sat in
the easy chair and stared at Anne. "You'll hurt the roots of
your hair. What's got you so upset?

"I'm not."

"You sure are."

Anne forced herself to lay down the brush and arranged
herself in a casual pose against the dresser, one that she
hoped hid her jealousy.

"Why didn't you tell me?" Madeline asked.

"Tell you what?"

"About Mark?"

"Why should I have?"

"Because he's terrific. I wouldn't have expected to find
a man like him in a place like this."

"I guess I hadn't noticed," Anne lied.

"You must be blind."

20

I wish I had been, Anne thought. *And I wish I were deaf so I couldn't hear you carry on about him!*

"By the way, what does one wear to the dunes?" asked Madeline.

"Jeans if it's chilly, shorts if it's not."

"I hope it's warm then."

"Why?"

"Because my legs aren't bad."

"Michigan weather's erratic," Anne warned. "It might be cold." *Please, be cold!* she thought.

"Mark's doing well for his age." Madeline changed the subject.

Would she ever quit?

"Really, to have one's own law practice at twenty-six is quite extraordinary."

"Yes, I guess it is."

"Of course it is!" Madeline paused. "Frankly, as far as I'm concerned, the more money a man makes the better."

How mercenary, Anne thought.

"I don't date poor men," Madeline affirmed, brushing off her skirt as if to sweep them away.

"Well, I do," said Anne. "Money isn't important."

"Quite the opposite. You're cloistered away in a Bible school and you don't understand life." She tossed her head to give emphasis to her next comments. "I'm accustomed to the best. When I marry, I'll marry a man who'll support me in the style to which I'm accustomed."

Anne frowned; Madeline was far more mercenary than she had thought.

Oddly, Anne's expression seemed to disturb Madeline. Her face softened and she said more mildly, "Of course, I'll make sure I love the man I marry."

The remark almost made Anne concede that Madeline wasn't entirely motivated by greed. But she couldn't—she was in no mood to be charitable.

Madeline rose and changed into a cream-colored night-gown that swept the floor and was as silky-smooth as the future she saw. "Mark would do nicely," Madeline said.

Stunned, Anne exclaimed, "To marry?"

"Exactly."

Marry Mark? No! But Madeline just might; she was the kind who accomplished what she purposed. Anne felt hysterical; she dashed to the bathroom, leaned against the sink, and wept.

Her own future was wrecked!

———

After Anne and Madeline turned in for the night, Anne tossed on a tear-damp pillow, while the old inn ministered creaks and groans and tense mouse scratches from the walls. Each return of the evening's events hurt more than the last. She must stop this! She had to sleep.

Hoping that a walk would quiet her thoughts and tire her, at 1:30 Anne slipped from bed, pulled on her jeans, and crept past her sleeping roommate. Outside, a sliver of moon was tipped behind a cloud and the air was cool on her face. No one was on the grounds. It was lovely and quiet and she felt a little better.

Anne walked along the path fronting the boathouse, heading for the beach. Several yards in the distance she heard an angry male voice. She stopped suddenly beside a support post, well out of the man's view.

"I'd suggest you drop that cold shoulder, honey," he barked.

"Shut up, you idiot!" came a woman's response.

"Don't give *me* orders. I'm coming to your room." The man had a precise, educated voice Anne didn't recognize.

The woman said, "You most certainly are *not*. You will please be on your way." The voice clicked like snapping fingers and held the hautiness of a medieval queen. Anne knew that voice; it belonged to Miss McGill.

Anne was amazed. By all appearances and actions, Miss McGill was a resolute spinster; yet she was with a man who had called her honey! A man bent on going to her room!

"I have my rights," said the man.

"After what you did tonight, you have no rights."

"Look, I said I'm sorry. I'm human. These things happen. It won't happen again."

"Remove your hand from my arm. You're hurting me."

Anne tensed. She knew she should leave, but felt riveted to the ground.

"Shut up!" he barked.

"Cheat!"

"Witch!"

"Fool!"

"We'll see who's a fool," he hissed.

Anne could hear a thump against the boathouse wall and Emma cried out. Another thump, and Emma whimpered. The man quickly disappeared into the darkness.

Oh, dear, he must have thrown Miss McGill against the wall. Anne started toward her, then stopped short at the end of the boathouse. If it were anyone else, she wouldn't hesitate, but because Miss McGill considered even polite inquiries intrusions of privacy, Anne decided to proceed with care. "It's Anne," she called out. "Are you all right, Miss McGill?"

"Go away!"

"Are you hurt?"

"No."

"But I heard you hit the boathouse."

"I didn't," she lied.

"But I'm sure I heard a thud—"

"You're mistaken—please leave!"

"But—"

"You're interfering, child!" Emma screeched. "Sneaking around, eavesdropping. Get out of here at once!"

But I was only trying to help, Anne thought as she hurried away.

5

*I*n the morning, Anne listlessly pulled up the back zipper of the uniform the inn supplied. With only a few hours' sleep, she was exhausted. *If today doesn't go better than yesterday, I'll surely collapse,* she thought.

Madeline was putting on her face, working from a huge case of makeup. *Just look at her,* Anne thought, as Madeline brushed on blush to lift her cheekbones. She was just the kind to make up like a movie star just to wait on tables.

Anne sighed. Well, she had more important matters to consider than Madeline's face. Difficult as it would be, she must apologize to Miss McGill for interfering last night, even though she didn't feel that she had really interfered. She simply had tried to help. But her intentions weren't important; what was important was that Miss McGill was angry with her. If she didn't smooth out their relationship, it would be extremely difficult to work here this summer.

Seven mornings a week Emma reported to her office at six o'clock to do her bookkeeping and correspondence. She was sure to be there now, and since Anne was several minutes early, she decided to take care of the apology now. She tied on a triangular black apron and said to Madeline, "I'm leaving now. I'll meet you in the kitchen."

"We've got plenty of time. Wait."

"I've got something to do before work." She wasn't about to explain her mission to Madeline.

Madeline dipped into a pot of eye shadow and rubbed

it on generously. Then outlined it with a darker shade on the
eyelid near the lash. Curious, Anne paused a minute to ask,
"Why do you use two colors?"

"It makes my eyes stand out." Madeline studied Anne.
I'll do your eyes for you later if you'd like."

"Thanks," Anne said, thinking that would be fun—until
she remembered her feelings about Madeline—"but I guess
maybe I'll leave them as they are."

Madeline shrugged. "If you change your mind, let me
know."

————————

Anne heard the rat-a-tat of Emma's typewriter as she
walked through the lobby and to the doorway of Emma's
office, a small room behind the front desk. Though the room
was paneled in knotty pine, there were so many bird prints
on the walls that the wood was barely visible. Like a sweet
note on an off-key piano, Emma had a spot of love amid all
her hostility, and that love she directed toward birds. Often
in her free hours she could be seen in the woods behind the
inn, stalking after them with her hands behind her back and
her binoculars around her neck. When Anne saw her bird-
watching, her heart always warmed and she would think:
Emma can't be all bad.

"Excuse me," Anne said softly.

Overreacting to the interruption, Emma's fingers
leaped from the keys and her chair swiveled around.

"I'm sorry I upset you last night," Anne ventured.

"You were eavesdropping." She glared at Anne.

"I wasn't. I was out walking—I overheard the com-
motion."

"Humph."

"Anyhow, I'm sorry."

"You didn't hear what you thought you heard."

"Then what was it?"

"You heard me rehearsing a poem for next week's bird society meeting. It's a poem in which a man and woman are in disagreement about a bird sighting."

Why did she lie? Was she too proud to admit she had been struck by a man?

Though Anne had come to apologize, not to discuss last night's events, she couldn't help but ask, "Then how did you come to fall into the boathouse?"

Emma didn't appreciate the question. She folded her arms over her broad chest. "It was a raccoon, Anne."

Emma's chair rolled toward Anne, and she added disdainfully, "You have an incredible imagination. Last summer you appeared in my office with the wild story that a child had fallen overboard. As you most certainly must recall, it wasn't a child that fell, but an oar. You created all kinds of ruckus around here for nothing."

"The boat was far from shore. Anybody would've thought it."

"Not anybody, Anne, just you. Just one who's given to flights of fancy. Frankly, I believe you need a psychiatrist, and if you repeat last night's episode to anyone, I shall make my opinion known."

Distraught over the tack the conversation had taken, Anne made one last attempt to smooth out their relationship. "Will you accept my apology?"

In a penciled voice that wrote an end to the conversation, Emma said, "All right—but from now on I expect you to keep our association on a businesslike level. You will never inquire into my affairs, as I will never inquire into yours."

The chair wheels spun and Emma was back to her typing.

6

*A*nne pushed through the swinging doors and was met with the rich smell of bacon and coffee.

Nobody but Tessie McGill would have such a kitchen. The walls, ceiling, and cabinets were enameled orange, and the floor was covered with glossy yellow linoleum. Tessie had once told Anne that she had chosen the dazzling colors because she liked to feel as if she were outside when she was inside. "You know, like I'm on the beach," Tessie had said.

When Tessie saw Anne, she threw up her stubby arms. She was short and round as a beach ball and she seemed to roll along as she came calling, "Anne." Her cheeks blazed with excitement, her pink uniform flapped, but her fuzzy auburn hair was stiff and still. To keep it neat while she worked, Tessie always sprayed it several times with super-hold hairspray. "Darling," Tessie swooned, as she took Anne into her arms.

Anne hugged her tightly. She loved Tessie almost as much as she had loved her mother.

"We tried to get back, but we couldn't," Tessie explained. When Tessie was excited she spoke abstrusely.

"Do you mean last night?"

"Of course. But how could we walk out? It was the annual Reily Gourmet Club banquet, and Jim's president this year."

"You couldn't," Anne said as Jim McGill swept her from Tessie, giving her a big hug.

"It's good to have you back," Jim said softly. He was tall and dark like Mark, but far quieter, happiest when he was cooking on his eight-burner stove.

Next Mark's brother Kevin hugged Anne, and shy Little Uncle (he operated the dishwasher) pranced around the edges, waiting for his chance to greet her.

Anne was very moved, loving them all.

Moments later Madeline arrived and Anne introduced her to the McGills. After they had welcomed Madeline heartily, Anne took her to the dining room, a narrow room with mullioned windows in the front and a fireplace and buffet table in the rear. All the meals were served from the buffet.

Anne pulled open the drawer in a large cabinet, lifted out a stack of place mats, and handed half to Madeline. "Our job's to set the tables and put on water glasses. When the guests have their food, we bring them their drinks. When they're finished eating, we clear the tables and set them up again. We keep the trays of food on the buffet filled. It's easy."

Madeline looked bored. "So I see."

Anne added defensively, "Actually, it's not that simple. We've got to be attentive to the guests and make them happy."

"Don't get nervous, I realize that." Madeline looked around. "Does Mark eat here?"

"Yes."

"How nice. What time does *he* get in?"

"About seven," Anne said, hurrying away to avoid the conversation.

If *he* was going to be Madeline's sole topic of conversation this summer, maybe she should quit. The Blue Hole, a restaurant in Reily, had advertised for a waitress—she could work there. But Anne loved her job at the inn. She loved Mark's family (except for Emma). No, she wouldn't let Madeline drive her away!

————

Mark filled his plate with the usual fare: scrambled eggs, grapefruit, two hot rolls. He seldom varied his selection. He sat near the buffet, leaving the more desirable front tables for the guests. He ate absently, his thoughts on Hazel Green, a meek little widow who kept her eyes on her shoes when she spoke. About nine months ago Hazel had suffered a stroke. Though she had made a fairly good recovery, her left arm and leg were still quite weak, and she didn't have the strength to resume her taxing work as a motel maid. She had long ago used her last dollar, but her only child, a married son in Reily, refused to give her financial assistance. "I've got my own worries," he had told Hazel coldly.

Mark had heard about Hazel through a client. The client and Mark had each given Hazel three hundred dollars, and Mark was trying to find light cleaning work for her. He had suggested she consider another line of work, but she had said, "I gotta clean. That's all I know, sir."

Mark had grown fond of Hazel and he wouldn't rest easy until she worked again. *Perhaps Mom has some light work Hazel could do in the kitchen,* he thought.

He finished his coffee, and Madeline poured him a fresh cup. "You're up early," she said.

"I usually work weekends. I was reading a contract before I came down." His goal was to have the largest law practice in the county in five years, and he believed he would have it.

"Then I feel honored you're taking time off for me," she said with a flirtatious flutter of her eyelids.

"I don't work all the time," he said flatly. He didn't care for overt flirting.

"Well, of course not," she said with another flutter of her eyes.

"How's the waitress work going?" he asked.

"Fine. It'd be almost fun if it weren't for that monster." Madeline frowned at a squealing boy in a highchair. "Look at that!" she exclaimed as the boy poured a glass of milk on his highchair tray. "The little brat! I suppose I've got to clean it up."

Mark laughed at her dramatics. "I'm afraid so."

While Madeline hurried to the kitchen for a cloth, he sipped his coffee and noticed that the Comptons were shouting louder than usual. They were at the same window table they had occupied for the last sixty years. They were thin as wires and both so deaf they shouted at others and others had to shout to them. Neither felt the need of hearing aids, however. "We hear just fine," they would shout. Though kind and apologetic, they were constantly sending the waitresses for hotter potatoes, firmer eggs, crisper rolls. Through the years, they had irritated scores of waitresses, but Anne didn't seem to mind them. "More coffee?" Anne raised her voice.

"No, dear," Mrs. Compton hollered while her sparrowy hand hovered over Mr. Compton's plate. "Just some jam for him. The strawberry. And he likes it thick, if you don't mind, dear."

"I'll get it right away," Anne complied.

"You'll be sure it's thick."

"I will," Anne said with a smile.

She's a sweet girl, Mark thought.

He stopped Anne on her way to the buffet table. "The Comptons have been eager for you to get here. You're their favorite waitress."

"That's nice," Anne said in a monotone.

She seemed depressed. To lift her, Mark invited her

again to climb the dunes. "Surely whatever you've got to do can wait an hour or so."

She frowned. "I'm afraid it can't."

"I'm disappointed. We've got a lot of catching up to do."

She flushed and said hotly, "What do you mean, catching up?"

"Well, it's been a long time."

"You could've stopped by school. It's only six blocks from your office."

"I didn't think of it. I've been busy."

"Then if it wasn't important enough to think about, it isn't important enough to catch up on," she blurted and hurried away.

Her strange behavior amazed him. Why would she expect him to visit her at school? They were simply casual friends. Unless . . . was it possible that she had read more into their friendship than was there? Had she interpreted his brotherly teasing as romantic interest? No doubt.

Resolving to be more careful in the future, Mark left to work in his room. At his desk, an image of Anne came to his mind. He smiled and returned to his papers.

———

Anne busied herself filling the salad dressing containers at the buffet table, careful not to look at Mark as he left the dining room. She'd never look at him again. Why had she lost her composure? Now Mark knew she cared for him. If only she could start the morning over again!

7

*U*nfortunately, the day was warm, and right now Madeline's lovely legs were striding toward the dunes in short jean shorts. *I don't even care*, Anne thought, slumping in the easy chair and propping her feet on Madeline's bed. She was exhausted. Everything was going wrong. Madeline and Mark were together, and probably discussing the fact that Anne obviously had a schoolgirl crush on Mark.

This was turning into the worst day of her life!

She hadn't felt so bitter in a long time. She paused, startled by the feeling, and admitted the extent of her jealous feelings toward Madeline. She felt removed from the Lord, whom she loved, but she knew why: her jealousy. Isaiah 59:2 was very much in her mind: ". . . It is your sins that separate you from God when you try to worship him."

"Forgive me, Lord," she whispered. And she knew He had.

"Help me to like Madeline, Lord."

Anne rose and started to rearrange her dresser so that she could put her jeans in the bottom drawer. When she had fitted them in, it dawned on her: *Madeline didn't know I loved Mark, so naturally she felt free to date him.*

I guess I really don't mind her so much, Anne decided.

She felt better. She knew she should talk to God about Mark—but she just couldn't—not yet. She refused to even think about him. She was afraid she'd get hysterical if she did.

———

While Anne and Madeline worked the lunch period, Madeline told Anne that the dune climb had been a religious experience. "I never had a pure feeling like that on State Street in Chicago," she said. And Mark was more wonderful than she had originally thought, "Absolutely marvelous."

Anne fought to keep her hands from her ears. She wasn't jealous of Madeline anymore, but she was still too in love with Mark to stand there listening. "That's wonderful," she said, and ran off to fill the guests' water glasses.

After lunch, Madeline went to the beach and Anne took the week's grocery invoices to Emma. Normally Tessie took them, but she was busy making cakes.

Emma was at the far end of the front desk, and before going to her, Anne stopped to talk to Rick Hobert, a desk clerk who was a chemistry major at the University of Michigan. He had worked here last summer and he and Anne had become close friends. "Hey, it's good to see you," Anne said. "I thought you wouldn't be here this summer. Didn't you have to work at your dad's paint company?"

He smiled, then nervously plucked at his blond mustache. He was bony, and the thick glasses he wore made him look like a hungry owl. "I decided not to. Dad didn't approve, but I came anyhow. I need to get my independence."

He leaned his sharp elbows on the counter. "What would you have done, Anne?"

"I don't know." She definitely believed that a child should obey his parents. But then, she had intended to date Mark, knowing that her father would disapprove.

"I really don't feel good about it," he said worriedly. "Maybe I've made a mistake and should go home."

"Maybe you should, then."

"But I don't *want* to," he said uncertainly.

When Rick became wishy-washy, he tended to vacillate

between his options for days. Anne doubted he would take her advice, but she tried anyway. "Maybe you should call your dad and straighten it out."

"Maybe you're right," he said.

Anne left and set the invoices down before Emma. "Tessie asked me to bring them."

"Mrs. McGill, if you please!" Emma snapped. "You will from now on refer to Mother using her surname."

Anne sighed. The trouble she had expected had already begun.

Emma snatched up the invoices. "Are these all there are?"

"I'm not sure. I don't know how many there're supposed to be."

"Hmm," Emma snorted, clearly indicating that if Anne had some sense she would know how many there should be.

"I'll go ask Tes—Mrs. McGill."

"Don't bother. I'll do it," Emma said.

Emma's attention went to a burly man, walking stiffly toward them as if having trouble keeping his legs on course. He was about forty and would have been quite attractive if his face weren't as red as a spoiled tomato. A screwdriver was shoved between his jeans and a leather belt with a horse-head-shaped buckle, from which zircon eyes shone large as marbles. The gaudy buckle and the cocky tilt of his head made Anne think he was the kind of man who would swagger if he could walk more steadily.

Is the man drunk? Anne wondered.

He stopped directly before Emma and she stepped back, greeted him, and reluctantly introduced him to Anne. He was John Blake, the new handyman. His predecessor had quit this last winter. John gave Anne's figure an appreciative glance, which made her blush, but he quickly went on to speak to Emma. He was nervous, defensive. "Don't say it . . . I'm aware I'm late checking in. I've been trying to tape that rotten section of hose, but the tape won't hold. I've got to replace the section."

He had enunciated each word, a bit like Miss McGill did. For a moment his voice simply seemed familiar, but then Anne recognized it. This was the man Miss McGill had argued with last night. This man, then, was her boyfriend. It was difficult to match him with Miss McGill; but then it was difficult to match any man with her. Why would she be attracted to him? He seemed an educated man, perhaps not working in a job suitable to his education. Maybe Miss McGill hoped to bring out his potential.

Emma frowned. "You're not driving to town just for that."

"The flowers need water. I can't reach them without another section."

"All right. You've made your point, but I'll pick it up myself when I go to town." Emma handed him a list of items needing fixing. "The bathtubs are at the top of the list. They've got to be fixed—*now*, not tomorrow, mind you, but *now*."

The man shoved the list in his pocket and Emma said, "Anne, why are you hanging around?"

She was surprised to realize she was. She supposed it was curiosity about their relationship that had made her stay.

"Don't go," John said, admiring her again with his eyes.

"The girl's got her duties," Emma said, giving him a proprietary glance.

Anne left as directed. She didn't appreciate John's scrutiny. She hated being eyed like that and she planned to keep her distance this summer.

Anne changed into the white shorts she had worn that morning and went to visit Tessie, who was still baking. Tessie's chubby arms were up to the elbows in flour. Large earthenware bowls of sliced apples and shucked pecans sat on the shelf above her worktable. Tessie made all the desserts served at the inn, and she considered herself one of the best, if not the best, bakers in Michigan. Therefore she hung a wooden sign over the buffet table that read: "Tessie the cook made the dessert that you took."

Fearing the poem didn't adequately express her pride in her baking ability, Tessie had been trying for some time to write another. But because she couldn't properly describe the pride she felt, she wasn't satisfied with her results. "I'll get it yet, though," she often told Anne.

"Pull up a stool," Tessie told Anne. "I've finished my cakes and I'm making my pies."

"Can I help?"

"No, darling, you've got enough with the meals. Just sit."

Anne sat and after they had visited awhile, Tessie said sadly, "I suppose you've noticed how run down the place is?"

"Well, as a matter of fact, yes."

"It's never been this bad. It's because of the new handyman. He's awful . . . just terrible."

"I just met him."

"What did you think?"

"Well—" Anne hesitated at saying what she thought.

"Then, you know?" Tessie exclaimed, looking upset.

Anne nodded.

"You must put it from your mind . . . forget what you know."

Tessie hated to think about the sordid, the wretched, even the disagreeable things in life. Normally she would have been quiet at this point, but her months of frustration exploded. "He's an alcoholic. Because of him we've got six stopped-up bathtubs and the guests are having fits. Last week he ruined my tulips—fell off the banister and smashed the red and white striped ones, the best color."

"Why do you keep him on?"

Tessie ran a floury hand across her forehead, leaving white smudges over her troubled eyes. "Because Jim and I like to give a person a chance—but he's about had his last. I can't tell you any more. It just isn't right for a minister's daughter to hear."

"But my dad's told me a lot about the alcoholics he's counseled."

"This is different."

"How could it be?"

"It just is," Tessie said adamantly. "I shouldn't have said what I did."

Anne gave up. She wondered where Tessie had developed her opinions as to what a minister's daughter should and should not hear. Certainly not at church, because Tessie never went. "I don't have time for all that," she once told Anne. "I'm right with God. I live a good life and the good Lord will take me to heaven when my time comes." When Anne tried to explain that salvation wasn't based on good works, Tessie interrupted with, "It's not good to discuss religion. It's much too personal."

Tessie fitted a circle of dough into a pan and said, "Did you pass your courses, Anne?"

Last year Tessie had driven in occasionally to visit Anne at school, and last week she had asked Anne to phone immediately upon getting her grades. "Yes, but I didn't call because I just got my grades yesterday. I was planning to tell you last night, but you weren't here."

"You promised to phone—you should have immediately."

Anne smiled. "Okay, next time I will."

"Now, what did you get?"

"Mostly A's."

Tessie smiled as she fluted the pie crust.

At ten o'clock that evening Anne was alone and very aware of the fact.

She was on the pier, in line with the path of moonlight on the water and probably in line with Madeline and Mark who were up on the dunes again. But they were far above her and it hurt to imagine how the spot she occupied would be only black space to them.

Her eyes filled with tears. To get her mind off Mark, she decided to walk to the overlook, a weedy, cracked slab of concrete about half a mile down shore. The overlook had once fronted the Piney Ridge, a rambling frame hotel built in 1850, another of the luxury resorts of its day. Unfortunately, the place was a firetrap and thirty years ago it had burned to the ground. The foundation was now beneath the sand and the only trace of the hotel was the overlook.

Anne could either walk along the shore or take the overland path. Deciding for the shore walk, she kicked off her shoes, rolled up her jeans, and jumped down into the water, her shoes in her hand. Because the overlook was on a high bluff, she would need them when she climbed it.

Halfway to the overlook she came to the Rosses' cottage, the last of the cottages she would pass. Ahead lay sand-faced bluffs, hung with arm-like cedar roots and topped with trees.

Anne began to forget Mark and enjoy the walk. The cool water felt good on her feet, the June air soft and just right on her face. Then about fifty yards before the overlook, everything changed.

A deep-pitched scream ripped the air, all the more terrifying because it was the scream of a man. The hair raised on Anne's arms. She hastily scanned the beach and the outer rim of the overlook. To the right, not far from where the forest met the concrete, a figure was darting toward the trees. It was a woman, wearing a white dress with billowy, long sleeves.

"Hey!" Anne shouted.

No answer.

"What's happened?"

No answer.

The woman disappeared in the trees. Surely she had heard Anne call. Why hadn't she stopped? Where was she going? Something awful had happened, Anne was sure of it. She squinted toward the beach and thought she saw a dark mound. Could it be the man? The guardrail around the overlook had rusted out in spots . . . maybe the man had fallen through. Maybe the woman was running after help. But if the man had fallen, why had she left without checking him?

Wondering only briefly, Anne was off running.

She sprinted diagonally through the water toward the beach. Her jeans were soaked and her shoes slipped from her hands, but she didn't stop for them.

The dark mound took a human shape. And when Anne finally stood over him, she knew immediately who he was. In horror she took in each detail.

One arm was flung over a piece of driftwood, and one foot was in the water, jostling up and down under the small waves. His head was turned awkwardly to the right, the result of a broken neck. His jeans clung to his legs. The two big eyes on his horse-head buckle gleamed in the moonlight. It was the handyman.

He looked like a broken puppet, and even before Anne bent down to feel for a pulse, she knew he was dead.

8

Oh, God, my dear Lord, Anne thought over and over as she raced along the overland path toward the inn. Just this morning John was alive. How could he be dead? Though she was aware that pine cones cut her feet, she was too shocked to feel pain. When she got to the inn, she ran up the veranda stairs and headlong into Mark. He took hold of her arms and steadied her.

His broad shoulders were before her. She longed to fall against him, wrap herself in his arms, have him comfort her. Then she remembered the embarrassing episode in the dining room. If she even touched him, he'd think she was expressing her affection for him. Her breathing was heavy. Tears spilled now for the first time. "What is it?" Mark asked anxiously.

"John Blake."

Madeline came then. "Good grief—you're a mess!" she exclaimed, looking from the wet jeans hugging Anne's legs to her bare feet and disheveled hair. "Let me take you in."

"No, no, not yet."

"Anne, what happened?" Mark demanded.

"John's dead."

"From what?" Mark said.

Madeline interrupted, "Who's he?"

"The handyman."

"The dark man with the odd belt?"

"Yes," Mark said, giving Madeline an impatient glance.

He asked Anne again. "What happened to John?"

While she wiped tears with the back of her hand, Anne told them what she had heard and seen.

"That's terrible," Madeline said matter-of-factly, not about to feign regret over the death of a stranger.

"Are you sure John's dead?" Mark asked Anne.

"He didn't have a pulse."

"A pulse can be missed."

"I'm sure of it. He wasn't breathing and it looks like his neck's broken."

Mark's face was grim. "How awful. We'd better call the police."

Anne took a few hobbled steps. The shock was over, and the cuts on her feet were painful. "Let me see those," Mark said and lifted her to the banister.

"They're not badly cut, but they need to be treated," he said. "After we call the police, go see my mom."

He lifted her down and put his arm around her to help her along. He was too near. She drew away. "I can walk by myself."

Dewey Clark, a junior at Florida State University, was on duty at the front desk. He was from northern Michigan and had gone south to school to escape the cold winters. Everything about Dewey was average, except his melancholy, which he had in abundance. Last summer, his second summer as a desk clerk at the inn, he had nicknamed himself Weedy. "It's my name, just spelled in another way," he often explained.

Anne saw Weedy's eyes on her. She knew what was coming. "Hey, barefoot," he called.

Anne greeted him, and while Mark phoned the police, she told Weedy what had happened. He was very upset and his words tumbled out. "Why, I just saw John in the parking lot this evening. He was dead drunk. I knew I should've made him go to his room. I shouldn't have let him wander off." He held his head in his hands. "To think I could have done something."

"You couldn't have known what was going to happen."

"In the hotel business a person's got to be perceptive. They've got to know everything," he said, and rushed to the other end of the counter to check in a guest.

Mark hung up, then went to tell his family about John. Immediately upon hearing the frightful news, Tessie flew to Anne, her fuzzy hair unlacquered and standing on end, her frayed chenille robe gaping, revealing green pajamas. "How awful that you had to be the one to find John's body!" she exclaimed, clasping Anne in her arms.

"Really, I'm okay." That was a partial truth; Anne felt better, but not completely over the shock. But Tessie was a wreck and would surely collapse if Anne showed any visual signs of distress.

"You're not okay, Anne." She held her at arm's length. "I can tell by your eyes."

Anne forced a smile.

"Mark says you've cut your feet."

"Just a little."

"Oh, you poor dear!" Tessie exclaimed, rushing Anne to her first-aid box in the kitchen.

Anne hoisted herself onto a kitchen counter and Tessie washed her cuts with soap and water. Tessie was almost overcome with guilt. "You know, I had such bad thoughts about John," she moaned. "Do you suppose I unconsciously wished his death?"

"Well, even if you did, you weren't the cause of his death," Anne assured her.

"Oh, dear Lord, bless his poor soul!" Tessie gasped.

Madeline had arrived to see if she could help. Her eyes expressed concern. Anne was surprised; she hadn't thought Madeline capable of concern for anyone besides herself.

"Hand me the alcohol, dear," Tessie spoke to Madeline.

As she dabbed the alcohol on the cuts, Tessie addressed Anne, "Have you called your father?"

"No, but I will when you finish here."

"Good—and when the police get here, I want *you* to stay in your room."

"But, how can I, Tessie? I'm a witness."

Tessie sighed. "I suppose so. But at least go upstairs and change into dry clothes."

After Tessie had applied several bandages to Anne's feet, Anne changed into dry jeans and went to the lobby, where, at the request of the police, Mark had gathered the family and staff.

Everyone was present except Emma. "She'll be right along. She stopped in the dining room for a cold drink," Mark said.

Anne sat down, and a moment later Sergeant Marcum arrived. He was old, thin, and exhausted looking. His eyes were bloodshot and the skin on his face sagged. He sighed as he dropped into a straight-backed chair. "Is everyone here?"

"Everyone but my sister," Mark said with a look toward the hallway. "She's just coming now."

Emma drifted across the room, decidedly lacking her usual briskness. She wore a long-sleeved white dress which was anything but fresh and neat. Several strands of hair were pinned hastily into her bun. Emma was always so meticulous, Anne thought—but then, of course, it was practically the middle of the night by now. She must have hastily dressed to meet with the police officer.

Then again, the dress looked vaguely familiar to Anne. Why, of course! The woman Anne had seen fleeing through the forest wore a white dress. She stifled a gasp at the thought. *But if it really was Emma, why would she leave the scene when she surely had heard John scream out?*

There were so many possibilities tumbling over in

Anne's mind. Perhaps Emma really loved John and became helpless at the thought of his certain death, having fallen from such a height. If this were so, how terrible she must feel now—how guilty and alone—if only Miss McGill weren't so difficult to get close to. Anne longed to comfort her.

9

Sergeant Marcum took a notebook from his pocket, poised his pencil, and said to Anne, "Tell me exactly what you saw at the overlook, young lady. And I mean *exactly*—don't speculate. You'll only waste my time if you speculate."

Anne carefully gave her account, fully expecting when she had finished that Emma would offer hers. But she didn't; her eyes were wandering around the room. Had she even been listening?

Sergeant Marcum asked, "Did you recognize the woman?"

"Well, not really. I—"

"I asked for exactness, and that includes exactness of opinion."

Anne hesitated, expecting Emma to speak up. When she didn't, Anne prompted her. "Sergeant Marcum is asking about the woman at the overlook."

"Hmm," was all Emma uttered and Anne decided she must be too shocked to speak.

Sergeant Marcum frowned, irritated. "I'm speaking to you, lady, not her. Did you recognize the woman or not?"

Anne had no choice but to speak out what she had seen and felt. "I—I think it was Miss McGill."

"You, Emma!" Tessie exclaimed. "You poor darling! It must've been awful."

Emma came alive with Anne's declaration. "I really don't know, Mother," she said crisply, "because I wasn't there."

"Then why would Anne say you were?"

"I have no idea," she returned dryly.

"Why do you say she was, Anne?" Tessie asked, becoming more and more flustered by the minute.

"Because I thought it was her. I guess I can't be positive. It was dark except for the moon."

Sergeant Marcum sighed, not happy with the confusion. He addressed Emma. "Were you at the overlook?"

"I was not. I was in my room, except for a very short period when I was out back listening to the screech owls. In fact, I just came in a few minutes ago."

Emma continued angrily. "You can be sure I know where I have and have not been. Furthermore, John was nothing but a drunk and I don't wish to be associated with a drunk."

"But I saw a woman in a white dress, and yours is ripped and dirty, Emma—er, uh, Miss McGill." Anne was becoming more and more convinced that Emma was indeed at the overlook.

Emma interrupted and spoke sarcastically. "Really, aren't you observant. I caught my dress on a branch out back. At this point, I think Sergeant Marcum ought to be made aware that you have trouble distinguishing what is from what isn't, Anne." She proceeded to relate the oar incident to Sergeant Marcum.

Anne fumed. Nobody would try that hard to discredit somebody's story unless she were lying. Now she was sure that Miss McGill had been at the overlook. "From where I was, the oar looked exactly like a child," Anne said.

Sergeant Marcum made no comment, and Anne wished she could retrieve her words. She hoped he wasn't constructing an analogy with them: the child is to the oar as the woman is to the— He pushed his weary body from the chair and crooked his finger at Anne. "Let's go. I need you to identify the body."

Anne was exhausted, upset, unable to cope with this impatient old sergeant. She forgot how hurt she was over Mark and Madeline. She needed him; he'd help her cope with Sergeant Marcum. "Can't Mark come? He's a lawyer. Don't I need a lawyer?"

"No," Sergeant Marcum said impatiently. "Come on."

Anne's eyes appealed to Mark, and he said, "Would you mind if I came along, Sergeant?"

"I'd mind. I don't need a lawyer muddling up my investigation."

Before Sergeant Marcum and Anne left, he requested that the family and staff wait in the lobby for further questioning.

Sergeant Marcum parked the squad car on the lane behind the overlook. The stairs down to the beach had long since rotted out, and though Anne was young enough to negotiate the slope on her feet, the old sergeant stumbled and jerked and finally slid down the slope. He cursed continually, and by the time he reached the beach, the pouches under his eyes made him look like an angered bloodhound. "Your handyman picked a lousy spot to plunge. If I'd known, I'd have had them send Harry. Believe me, Harry's got his coming."

He snapped on a five-cell flashlight and ran the beam over John's body. The horse-head eyes shone and Anne looked away. "Is this John Blake?" he said matter-of-factly. What was a gruesome chore for Anne was a routine matter for him.

"Yes."

"Is this exactly where you left him?"

Anne glanced again at John. "Yes."

Sergeant Marcum turned John onto his stomach, reached into the back pocket of his jeans, and pulled out a red and gold whiskey label, from which hung strips of jagged glass. He dropped the label into a plastic bag, then photographed John's body.

Unwilling to disturb him, Anne waited until he had finished searching John, the beach, and the overlook to say, "I really do think it was Miss McGill I saw here."

"I don't. But even if it was, I doubt we'd prove it. The overlook's concrete . . . an elephant couldn't leave a print. There's nothing on the ground—not even a scrap of paper. It's her word against yours."

"Someone else might've seen her. You'll ask, won't you?"

"I'll ask," he said brusquely, "but if they had, they'd have probably volunteered the information when you brought it up. Moonlight's uncertain. You were quite a distance away; you might have seen a tree."

The analogy!

"But you saw the rip in her dress, sir."

"I believe she said she caught it on a branch."

"But the branch could have been at the overlook. Why do you take her word over mine?"

"I don't."

But he was.

An ambulance arrived, interrupting them. From Sergeant Marcum's conversation with the attendants, Anne learned that John would be taken to the morgue, where a medical examiner would perform an autopsy. "The guy had a pint of booze on him," Sergeant Marcum told the attendants. "In my opinion, he had a few too many and took a dive."

He is forming conclusions way to soon, Anne thought. Her head was spinning with questions for which she had no answers. There were connections she should be making, but she was too unnerved to think.

When Anne and Sergeant Marcum walked into the lobby, Anne tried not to notice how closely Madeline and

Mark were sitting on the couch. It would take a while to accustom herself to these scenes.

Anne sat down, and Sergeant Marcum began his questioning with Jim McGill, who said that John was 39, unmarried, and except for a brother in Grand Rapids, without any living family. John had arrived for his job interview in a battered Ford, with the story that he was tired of teaching English to unappreciative high school students. He wanted to switch to a more rewarding profession; maintenance work seemed a perfect choice. Jim believed he smelled liquor on John, and it occurred to him that John was an alcoholic who had been repeatedly fired and was after any job he could get.

But Tessie had insisted John be hired. She was charmed by his educated speech and his remark that he would like to paint the stairs to the beach yellow. "Wonderful—just exactly the right color," she had raved. Jim overlooked the liquor odor and hired John, reasoning that because of his own allergies he had a poor sense of smell. "I shouldn't have hired him," Jim said. "It turned out he was a poor worker—slow and undependable."

"He never painted the steps," Tessie said sadly. "He never did much of anything."

While Tessie's nervous glances revealed her concern for Anne's having to hear it all, everyone corroborated John's alcoholism, and Jim said that John often drank at the Whitefish, a dingy tavern by the docks in Reily. Often he brought home women, whom he entertained in his room over the garage. *Maybe they were fighting about one of them last night*, Anne thought.

Then Weedy, still feeling guilty about not having averted the tragedy, told Sergeant Marcum that he had seen John in the parking lot shortly before he died. "How was I to know he was headed off to die?" Weedy declared.

"You couldn't have known," said Tessie kindly. "Don't blame yourself."

"Was he with a woman in the parking lot?" Officer Marcum questioned Weedy.

"No—he was alone."

"Did anyone see him with Miss McGill—or with any other woman, perhaps one of the women from the White-fish?"

No one had. "Well," said Sergeant Marcum, looking matter-of-factly at Anne.

She guessed his thoughts: *If Miss McGill had been with John, surely someone at this busy place would have seen them leaving.* For some reason, he was not about to involve Emma in the incident.

Anne remained quiet, unable to think of a comment that would change his thinking. She was angry with him. She hated the fact that he simply discounted her story. If only she could talk to Mark—maybe later—explain her position, get his advice. But, of course, she couldn't. She couldn't bear to be close to him.

After Sergeant Marcum finished his inquiry, he searched John's room. He found nothing of special interest, except several whiskey flasks, which Anne supposed further confirmed his opinion that John had stumbled from the overlook in a drunken stupor. Before leaving, he asked Mark to pack up John's belongings and store them until John's brother could claim them.

10

I'll just sleep in my jeans, Anne thought, flopping on the bed and rolling herself up in the bedspread. She was too tired to slide under the covers. She had just called her father and reviewed the events of the evening, assuring him she was all right. That was the last task, and she was exhausted.

"You can't sleep like that!" exclaimed Madeline as she entered the room.

"Yes, I can; I'm too tired to undress."

"Just stand up and take off your jeans, Anne."

"I can't," she moaned.

Madeline marched to the bed and tugged off Anne's jeans, handing her a silk nightgown—one of her own from Berkshire's.

Touched by Madeline's care, Anne warmed to her. *I guess she can be kind of nice*, Anne thought.

After slipping on the gown, Anne climbed under her sheets and Madeline turned out the light. The silk gown felt cool and soft against her skin and she expected to drift off in seconds. But she didn't. An image of John on the beach came to her and she began shaking uncontrollably. *Don't think about it*, she commanded herself, forcing her attention on the storm just moving in—fastening her eyes on the draperies swelling under the breeze, listening to the thunder rumbling in nearer and nearer.

At the overlook she had been overwhelmed with questions, had sensed there were connections yet to be made.

Unconsciously, she must have been struggling for answers, because suddenly, when lightning flashed just beyond the window, she started to pull it all together. . . .

Emma claimed she wasn't at the overlook, yet Anne was almost certain she had been. After all, Miss McGill had tried to discredit her with that oar story. No, Anne decided, she wasn't *almost* certain Miss McGill had been at the overlook; she was positive. Every instinct confirmed that as a fact. So why hadn't Miss McGill admitted she was there? Had she lied to hide her involvement with John? Would that be sufficient reason for a lie of that magnitude? Wouldn't it have been more normal, even for an extremely decorous person like her, to admit she was there? She could have simply said she had taken a walk with John. She wouldn't have had to reveal any romantic inclinations.

Also, wouldn't she, unless she were covering up something, have gone for help when John fell? Yes! Undoubtedly, Miss McGill was hiding something. But what? Anne considered the fight she had overheard by the boathouse, where they had been possibly arguing about one of John's girl friends. What if they were having a similar argument at the overlook? What if in the midst of it, they fought, and John pushed her and she pushed him? He was drunk, he fell backwards, and tumbled from the overlook. Would that motivate Miss McGill to say she wasn't there, to run from the scene?

Far more chilling thoughts made Anne bolt upright. Miss McGill was capable of hate, and she had an unforgiving nature. What if she had been furious over a new girl friend? Or what if John had outright jilted her and she'd been wild with anger? What if, then, she had deliberately pushed John from the overlook. A terrible conclusion. Impossible!

But, was it?

No, it was entirely possible, Anne decided. Indeed very likely that Miss McGill either accidentally or deliberately pushed John. There could be no other reason Miss McGill would cover up the fact that she had been with him.

What should she do? Dare she call Sergeant Marcum with her conclusions when he had discounted her all along? Yes, she had to. She recalled a scripture she had studied in Bible school last year, Proverbs 17:15: "Acquitting the guilty and condemning the innocent—the Lord detests them both." She must do whatever was necessary to uphold justice.

———

In the morning, though Anne's feet felt much better, Tessie insisted she rest and tucked Anne's covers tightly around her. She called in a part-time waitress from Reily. Anne had slept little during the night and she immediately fell asleep, not waking until Madeline returned from working breakfast.

Since Anne's conclusions about Emma were shattering, she thought it only right to share them first with Sergeant Marcum. Therefore, she phoned him from the booth in the front hall, where Madeline wouldn't overhear their conversation. He was not at the station, but she reached him at home. "You're interrupting my breakfast!" he snapped.

"But it's important, sir."

"Well, I certainly hope so."

"I think Miss McGill was responsible for John's death."

A heavy sigh like the wind blew through the receiver. "Explain, then," he said.

Anne related the conclusions, beginning with the fight beside the boathouse, and finishing with the idea that Emma had either accidentally or deliberately pushed John from the bluff in the midst of an argument over a girl friend.

"Ridiculous!" he barked when she had finished. "One conjecture after the other. If I conducted my investigations on the basis of wild imaginings, I'd have the President of the United States involved here."

This man was impossible! she thought. "But I know what I heard by the boathouse. I—"

"Look, John was an alcoholic. He was doing what alcoholics do—drinking. John was drunk, he fell. The autopsy'll prove he was plastered."

"But even if it does, that doesn't mean John wasn't pushed."

"What are you," he croaked, "some kind of female Sherlock Holmes?"

"No, but—"

"Call me when you've got some *facts*," he interrupted, and hung up.

Furious with him, Anne marched away. She knew she was right and he was wrong. What should she do? Should she explain her opinion to another officer on the force— maybe Harry?

She saw Mark coming down the stairs. Not him! Not now! She could barely cope with the phone conversation, much less the feelings his presence brought.

He set his briefcase beside the bottom stair and greeted her, while she concentrated on not noticing how strikingly handsome he looked in his gray pinstripe suit. Though it was Sunday, he apparently was headed for work. Anne wasn't surprised; like Tessie, he never attended church. For him Sunday morning was the same as any other day of the week.

"How are your feet?" Mark asked.

"Pretty good."

"And you?"

"Okay, I guess."

Mark studied her. "You seem upset."

"I'm not." She refused to tell him about the phone conversation; he was the last person she would make her confidant!

She intended to leave, but was struck with second thoughts. Maybe Harry was as difficult as Sergeant Marcum. Maybe she did need to confide in Mark; he was a lawyer and he could tell her what steps she should take. But then, Emma was his sister. If she told him what she believed Emma had done, wouldn't he be hurt, or angry? Suddenly, though, the events of the last twelve hours crushed in on her, compelling her to share, and she told him exactly what she had told Sergeant Marcum. She ended by saying, "I'm really sorry. I realize I'm speaking about your sister."

"That's okay," he said quietly.

Was he hiding his feelings?

"Are you sure?"

"Yes. I suppose I have some love for Emma, but we're not that close. She's hard to get along with, and when I was a child she pinned things she did on me, getting me into trouble. I don't hold anything against her now though—I just tend to let her be. I can be objective about her."

"What should I do about my suspicions?"

"You've done all you can at this point."

"Do you believe I'm right?"

"I don't know."

"But I feel so *sure*."

"But you can't be. You've given a theory. Theories aren't facts."

Mark wasn't disregarding her entirely, and Anne ventured to ask, "Would you talk to Sergeant Marcum, explain my side of this? Maybe he'd pay some attention to you."

"I might, but I'd like to hear your story again before I decide." He glanced at his watch. "I've got to leave now for an appointment, but I could meet you around three."

"Fine."

"Will my room be all right?"

No! His room would be terrible. She'd faint if she were alone with him up there. *Tell him that!* she thought. But as if in a dream, he floated away while she nodded yes.

She must be crazy. She had to run after him, agree on another meeting place. No, she'd better leave well enough alone, she decided. Undoubtedly he considered his room his office. In reality she was like a client going to a lawyer. She'd have no trouble with her emotions, because every second she was in his room she'd remember that he and Madeline were crazy about each other.

11

*T*hough it was the first time Anne had been in Mark's room, she had always been aware of exactly where it was: on the second floor, three doors past the water cooler, on the left-hand side. His room was twice as large as hers and a wicker screen divided the sleeping area from the sitting area. The details of the room were obscured by the quantity of books that were crammed into shelves and piled on every possible surface, including a ragged-looking chair by the window.

Anne tucked her full skirt under her and sat on the couch. She was nervous and pressed close to the arm, which seemed to offer a measure of security. She was careful to remember how much Mark liked Madeline.

Mark opened a mini-refrigerator. "Would you like something to drink?" he asked.

"I don't drink," Anne said.

He laughed. "I mean a soft drink."

Embarrassed, Anne blushed. She should have known he meant a soft drink. The meeting was starting out all wrong! "No thanks," she said.

Mark opened a can of ginger ale for himself, moved the books from the worn chair, and sat down. Then at his prompting, Anne explained her theory as to how John died, only this time in greater detail than she had earlier. "What do you think?" she asked when she had finished.

"Give me a minute."

While he thought, Anne noticed that she was far more relaxed than when she had come in. If she was careful not to look directly into his eyes, he almost seemed like just a lawyer, and she just a client.

Finally Mark said, "Emma almost never wears a dress when she's out bird-watching or listening to owls. And a white one would seem even more inappropriate. What she usually wears is a pair of khaki pants. So that fact supports your theory that Emma was at the overlook."

As to Anne's theory of how John died, Mark believed it possible that Emma accidentally pushed John, even mildly possible she had deliberately done so. His face was grim as he added, "It's her cantankerous disposition that opens the possibility she acted deliberately. That and some of her past actions."

In explanation he related a recent incident. "Little Uncle (a lover of butterflies, a gentle man who netted them but never killed them) once netted a mourning cloak with a particularly brilliant border of yellow on its wings. Enchanted with the butterfly, he put it in a well-ventilated bottle and set it on a counter, where he could watch it while he worked. He was called away for several minutes, and when he returned he found the butterfly dead, pinned to a cabinet. When Little Uncle told me this story, those apple-like cheeks of his were wet with tears. 'Emma killed the butterfly,' he said. 'She told me she was helping me. She said I had to stop fiddling with butterflies and learn to kill and collect.' "

"That's terrible," Anne said.

"I think so too."

"Tell Sergeant Marcum *that* story!"

He smiled. "It may not be the right time for it."

"But you'll speak to Sergeant Marcum?"

"Yes," Mark said, "but I want you to stay open to his side. He may very well be right."

"But you just said my theory was plausible."

"Plausible isn't actual, Anne."

"In this case, I think it is."

"Anne," he laughed. "You *are* stubborn. And for a Bible school student!"

"One doesn't have anything to do with the other."

He laughed again, enjoying her for some reason she didn't understand.

Mark stood, indicating the interview was over. At the door she forgot herself and looked directly into his eyes. He was studying her most peculiarly. What was in his mind? She didn't know why, but she believed he liked something about her.

Enough of those thoughts! How had she managed to forget about him and Madeline? "Well, I'll be going," she said.

"I'll get back to you after I talk to Marcum," he said.

She left with a light feeling, as though a load had been lifted from her shoulders.

———

When Anne came into the room, Madeline was putting the last brush of polish on her nails. She draped her hands over the arms of the easy chair so that her nails would dry undisturbed. She never blew on them, she explained, because that might ruffle the polish.

"I'm bored," Madeline said. "Mark's out, but I'm hoping he'll get back so we can do something before dinner."

"He's back," Anne said and continued thoughtlessly, "I just left his room."

"You just left his room!" Madeline cried and her hands flew up, forgetting her polished nails.

"We were working on the case," Anne said hastily to calm her.

"The case? What case?"

"I mean we were discussing John's death."

Madeline scowled incredulously. "In his *room*?"

How ridiculous to have mentioned where she'd been. At any rate, with Madeline so upset she wouldn't try to explain her theory about John's death. "I was only there for a few minutes. It was a very businesslike discussion."

"Well, in my opinion, you should hold your meetings on the veranda," Madeline said with a long glare. "In his bedroom, indeed," she muttered.

12

*M*onday dawned chilly but clear with the sun working to warm the air. Though her feet hurt, Anne was on duty at breakfast. Tessie was upset about that and questioned Anne each time she walked into the kitchen. "I'm doing okay," Anne kept reassuring her.

Anne felt she had to work. Work would keep her mind off the murder and from her unnerving affection for Mark. She knew she should refer to the murder in her mind as the accidental death, but she couldn't seem to think of it that way.

Anne wore a cardigan, but Weedy, having trouble acclimating to Michigan weather, wore a pullover, a cardigan, and wool socks. "Boy, this is it," he told Anne, pausing on his way to have breakfast in the kitchen. "Next year I'm working in Miami. You should too."

Anne laughed. "I don't like hot weather."

Weedy switched to the matter foremost in his mind. "I should've known John was in danger."

"Everyone has told you that you couldn't have known."

"But I should have."

"No," Anne said and touched his hand, then regretted that she had when she saw the look in his eyes. He had asked her out repeatedly last year, but she had always refused. She liked him as a friend, but had no romantic feelings for him; he was too fretful, too hyperactive, too melancholic for her taste. Weedy always managed to find girls who would date him, so in reality he shouldn't be upset because Anne didn't. Exactly the opposite was true, however.

"You're so sympathetic," Weedy said.

"The Comptons need tea," Anne said, taking a step back.

"Wait." His eyes rested lovingly on her. "Come walking with me after dinner."

"I'm sorry, I can't."

"You always say no," Weedy said woefully.

"Then maybe you should stop asking."

"I'll never give up," he said with conviction.

Well, she certainly wouldn't be dating him; she wouldn't be dating anyone! After her letdown with Mark, she wouldn't have the heart for it.

———

That afternoon Tessie paused in her bread-baking to tell Anne that Jim had hired another handyman. He wouldn't room over the garage as John had, but in the hotel, where the family could keep an eye on him. "We're pretty sure he'll work out," said Tessie, "but after John, we've got to be careful." She then mentioned that Mark had asked her to hire Hazel Green, the needy widow. "We just can't," Tessie said sadly. "We just can't afford another house-keeper."

"My dad lost his housekeeper," Anne remembered, adding that she would ask him if he would hire Hazel.

Tessie's fingers trailed absently over the stiff ends of her fuzzy hair. "Well, Anne, when do you think Mark will start dating you?" she said. "You aren't discouraging him, are you?"

For two years Tessie had been hoping that Anne and Mark would get together; obviously she was upset that Mark was dating Madeline. "I don't know, Tessie. I guess we aren't each other's type."

"But you are, dear, you are!"

"No, I don't think so, Tessie," she countered.

"A mother knows."

"Tessie, he really likes Madeline. He'll probably marry her."

"Marry her!" She clutched her hair.

"Well, not right away." Anne tried to soften her statement.

"Certainly not! I know my boy. This is a fling."

Tessie plunged her fists into her bread dough, ending the conversation.

Anne left quietly, secretly hoping Tessie was right.

———

Late that afternoon Mark phoned Anne to arrange a meeting in his room at 9:45 P.M. to discuss his conversation with Sergeant Marcum. "I'm sorry to make it so late, but I've got a business dinner."

"Oh, fine, but maybe we should meet on the veranda."

"Does meeting in my room make you uncomfortable?"

She'd never admit that to him! "No—no, of course not."

"Then let's plan it there."

"Fine," she said.

When she hung up, she thought, *How did I ever agree to meet in his room again? If Madeline finds out, she'll be furious.*

At 9:30 Anne brushed her hair, hoping she could leave without Madeline questioning her. Madeline jumped from her bed and tossed down her book. "I've had it with reading. I'm sick of waiting for Mark to call. Last night I had to phone him for a date and I'm not phoning him again!" She scowled, making her pretty face very unbecoming.

She lit a cigarette and casually asked, "Why are you brushing your hair at this hour?"

"Well . . . I . . ." Why hadn't she combed her hair in the hall!

"Well, what?"

Anne couldn't lie. "I'm meeting Mark. It's about John's death again."

"Where are you meeting?"

If only she could lie! "In his room."

Red splotches erupted on Madeline's cheeks.

"I'll only be there a short time, Madeline. His office is in his room, you know."

"You're after him, aren't you?"

"Of course I'm not!"

Madeline scrutinized her. "Okay," she relented. "I believe you. Ask him to call me when you're finished with your business. I'm tired of waiting for him."

Ten minutes later, Anne sat exactly where she had sat the day before. She wore faded jeans, a green T-shirt with Reily Bible School written across the front, and beat-up running shoes. She had purposely worn old clothes to assure Madeline that she had no romantic interest in Mark. Now she wished she had worn something a little less casual. After all, she may never have another excuse for being alone with Mark.

Mark served Anne a soda, then told her that John's autopsy had been done yesterday and the laboratory work finished today. The toxicological test was negative, indicating John had not taken any drugs. The blood alcohol test revealed a level of .35 percent, an amount that would floor an occasional drinker, but that an alcoholic could manage—though just barely. Physically John was in good shape, ruling out the possibility he had suffered a heart attack and fallen from the bluff. John didn't write a suicide note, or give any indication he was depressed enough to jump. There was no evidence of foul play. Therefore, the medical examiner ruled that John's death was probably accidental, that he probably fell from the cliff in a drunken stupor.

Sergeant Marcum was pleased with the ruling and he closed the case. He wouldn't consider Anne's theory, nor any speculations about bird-watching pants and pinned-up butterflies. Because nobody had seen Emma or any other woman with John prior to the accident, he believed the man had surely been alone. He had told Mark, "Anne's got a detective complex. Tell her to mind her tables and I'll mind the station."

The statement brought out the fight in Anne. "He can't just close the case! What would make him reopen it?"

"Hear me out," Mark said, and explained that he had appealed to the district attorney, but it was his policy not to reopen cases closed by investigative officers. With that door closed, Mark returned to Sergeant Marcum and asked him what type of evidence would cause him to reopen the case.

"Well?" Anne asked.

"Evidence that Emma threatened to kill John, or strong indication that she had a motive to kill him. Or someone besides you to place her at the overlook. He wants strong evidence. He's old and he thinks he's got all the answers. He won't reopen the case unless he's forced."

"Then I'll have to look around," Anne said uncertainly. And she definitely would, even though it would be difficult. What would she look for? Witnesses? Letters? Notes?

"Look around for what?"

"For evidence."

"Why? Why not just forget it? What's in it for you?"

Anne looked levelly at Mark. Neither was he a Christian, nor, as far as she knew, did he read a Bible. She hoped he would understand. "I know Emma had something to do with it and I can't ignore that. I believe God would want me to uphold justice," she said softly.

Mark was giving her the same look of interest he had

given her at the door yesterday. Why? She had hardly said anything.

Loud shouts could be heard from the shuffleboard court. Mark shut the window and leaned casually against the wall. "I'll help you look," he said.

"But, why?" Anne looked puzzled. Hadn't he just said to forget it?

"We have to clear up the uncertainties. I am also convinced that justice should be upheld. I vowed when I became an attorney that I would fight violence and injustice, at the cost of any personal suffering or family ties. Besides, I believe justice comes from man, not God."

He was wrong, but she couldn't go into that. She must tell him that they couldn't investigate together, because Madeline would be furious. "Maybe I should just look for evidence myself."

"You wouldn't know how to go about it. This is far more along my line than yours."

Thoughtlessly, Anne blurted out, "But what would Madeline think?"

His voice was firm. "She won't think anything because she won't know. Nobody will know, because I don't want Emma to get wind of it."

She had started it, so she might as well finish it. "But, if Madeline sees us together, she'll have a fit. Before I came tonight, she asked if I had feelings for you."

He grinned. "Do you?"

"Of course not!" she said with as much indignation as she could muster.

He laughed, thoroughly enjoying himself. Anne jumped to her feet and stood before him. She must make him think he meant nothing to her. "Don't laugh," she said hotly. "It's Madeline who likes you, not me."

He just grinned again.

"She doesn't want me near you, and I can't look for evidence with you!"

"Of course you can. I've got nothing going on with her. We've had a few dates and she's fun, but that's it."

He wasn't wild about Madeline? The news rocked Anne. She could think of nothing except how close he was standing to her.

"Then I guess it's okay," she said sheepishly.

He bent and kissed her on the forehead, then stepped back. It had all happened in a second. She was totally unnerved. Was the kiss a seal of their agreement to investigate? "Why did you do that?"

He answered her question with his own. "Why do you suppose?"

He must like me, she thought, *at least a little bit*.

Suddenly he was all business again. He walked away, sat on his worn chair, and in a calm, clear voice started to sketch a plan for obtaining the kind of evidence Sergeant Marcum required. . . . They would search for physical evidence (notes, letters) and for testimony. To obtain testimony they would ask questions of the staff, family, deliverymen, guests, and so on. To guard against Emma learning of their investigation, they would ask their questions obliquely and they wouldn't divulge the purpose of the questions unless the person was about to give important testimony. In that case, the person would have to understand the necessity for secrecy. Mark suggested that tomorrow they search John's room and car. "Fortunately I've got a legitimate reason for going through John's things," Mark said. "I promised Marcum I'd pack them."

"Are you free after dinner tomorrow?" he asked Anne.

Anne nodded, vaguely taking in his words, but thinking about the kiss. He stood and led her to the door. "Oh, Anne," he said, "it might be a good idea to ask your dad if he minds your being involved in this search. He might have reason to be opposed to it."

"Oh, okay, I'll call him," Anne said.

Anne was outside the door when she remembered Madeline's request that Mark phone her. She told him.

"Fine," he said. "I need to phone her anyhow. I don't want you in a bad position over this investigation."

"What will you tell her?"

"That I'm not interested in her."

"Mark, she'll be hurt." Anne was shocked at his seeming lack of concern.

"Better now than later. She's acting very possessive, and she's only known me a few days!"

"She'll be hurt when she sees us together. Can't I tell her about the investigation?"

"No—and you don't need to go into any big explanations, either." With that he said good-night and shut the door.

So that was that. Madeline wasn't going to take this lightly.

13

*M*adeline stormed around the room like a tornado. "One hour is *not*, I repeat, is *not* a few minutes!" she railed at Anne. "What were you doing up there all that time with Mark?"

"I already told you we were talking about the circumstances of John's death."

"For an hour!" her voice shot up after the smoke from her long cigarette.

Anne kicked off her shoes and lay back on her bed. Determined not to panic, she shut her eyes and said nothing. If only she could explain about the investigation. As bad as the situation was now, it would be worse when Madeline learned Mark wasn't interested in her. And when she would begin to see Mark and her more and more together—Anne hated to think of the consequences.

"It took time to talk," Anne finally said.

"You're stretching my ability to believe you."

"Well—"

The phone rang. Madeline grabbed it and made a date to meet Mark in a few minutes. She was happier now, while she touched up her makeup and tucked in her blouse. "I'll keep him waiting a few minutes," she said, taking special pains with her hair. "After all, I waited an *hour* for him."

Finally, when she felt he had waited long enough, she left.

Anne then dialed her father and asked his permission

to investigate with Mark, carefully explaining the details of the case. He paused before answering, and she could imagine him in his study, wearing a plaid flannel shirt, because he always wore a flannel shirt when it was below seventy degrees. Except for that one small quirk, he was a logical man.

"Is Mark levelheaded?" Reverend Lindsey finally asked.

"Of course, Dad. You met him—you know that."

"Hardly. I've barely spoken to him." There was a pause. "Would this put you in any danger, Anne?"

"How do you mean?"

"Well, say Miss McGill *did* murder John. She might go after you if she discovers you're trying to implicate her."

"She won't know. We'll be very careful she doesn't."

"All right," he said. "But if you suspect any danger, go to the police."

"It's sixty-eight degrees, Dad," she said lovingly.

"Yes, honey—I'm cozy here in my plaid flannel," he said.

"I knew it."

Anne then told him about the widow, Hazel Green, and he agreed to interview her. With that, Anne hung up and waited in the easy chair for Madeline.

When she came in, she avoided Anne's eyes. She wandered pensively around the room while she changed into a nightgown. Finally Madeline said in a weary voice, "You knew, didn't you?"

Anne nodded and tried to convey with her eyes how badly she felt for her.

"I've never been rejected by a man before."

"I'm sorry, Madeline."

She slowly tied the sash on her robe, taking pains to even up the loops. When she had them just right, something seemed to snap inside and she tossed her head back and said defiantly, "This is the price I pay for becoming interested in a small-town man. Mark's simply not sophisticated enough to appreciate a person like me. Frankly, he's more your type, Anne."

Was she reading her mind? "You think so?"

"Well, don't you?"

"I guess so. Actually, I think he's pretty special."

"That's what I thought. If you cared for him, why didn't you say so?"

"Because of your own feelings for him."

"But you must have hoped he'd date you, not me."

"I guess I did."

"You never said a word, Anne."

"Because you liked him."

"How long have you been feeling this way?"

"Two years."

"You'd put aside two years of feelings because of *me*?" Madeline was amazed.

Anne nodded.

"That was decent of you," Madeline said with respect.

She then began vigorously brushing her hair, ending the conversation. There was a good feeling between them. For the first time, Anne felt they could possibly become friends.

———

The next evening at 7:10, five minutes before dinner service ended, Mark filled his plate from nearly empty bowls and trays and sat at his usual table by the buffet. Madeline approached, smiled with cool disinterest, and passed. Her pride was hurt, of course. But she was hardly a wallflower and she would forget him in a day or two and be on to somebody else. At the moment Mark was irritated with her. He hadn't appreciated waiting a half hour in the lobby for her the night before, only to tell she was no longer interested.

He watched Anne raise a full tray of dishes to her shoulder, balancing the load easily, even though she was slim and small-boned. She was well-coordinated, and he enjoyed watching her. Though ceiling fans ventilated the room, her forehead was flushed and damp from her work. She pushed through the kitchen doors.

Somehow she had matured over the winter and become an appealing young woman. It had taken an exercise of will the night before not to gather her into his arms. He admired her strong sense of justice, her fight, the fact that she had been willing to tackle the investigation alone. He remembered how disappointed Anne had been because he hadn't visited her at Bible school. During that conversation, he had worried that she might be romantically interested in him. Now he feared she wasn't.

When Anne returned to the dining room, Mark called her over and asked if they could get together at nine o'clock, after he had studied a few contracts for clients. Anne agreed, then asked him to phone her father, explaining that he was willing to interview Hazel Green.

"Of course," Mark said, delighted that Anne had taken the interest and initiative.

Anne smiled, and he returned it, sending her joyfully on her way.

After eating, Mark stopped at the front desk to pick up the keys to John's room before arranging for Hazel's interview. Rick Hobert was on duty. "I'm staying," he told Mark.

"Oh, where were you going?"

"Home—my dad wanted me at the paint company."

"I'm glad you'll be here." Mark believed Rick lacked backbone. Another summer on his own might give it to him. "Can I have John's keys?"

Behind his thick glasses, Mark could see Rick's frustration. He hated disappointing others. He was at everyone's service, even to the extent of going after soft drinks and coffee for the guests when he was off duty. "Miss McGill's got them. If you watch the desk I'll run up to her room and ask for them."

"I'll get them," said Mark. "Why did she take them?"

"She said she had to pack John's things. She said you'd be too busy and she thought she'd help you out."

Mark considered Emma's action. She never helped others; she couldn't have been motivated by a desire to help him. Rather, she had probably gathered up John's possessions in order to eradicate all evidence of her association with him. Last night he hadn't been totally convinced Emma was implicated in John's death, but now he was becoming more certain. On the outside chance Emma had overlooked something, he and Anne would go ahead with their search.

Emma lived in the tower, not far from Anne's room. Both Anne's room and the stairway to the tower were in a short ell off the third-floor corridor. Emma answered Mark's knock, invited him in, and motioned to a teapot on a small dining table fitted against one of the tower's angled walls. "Tea?" she asked.

He shook his head. "I've come for John's keys. Rick told me you've packed his things, but I want to make sure everything's in order."

"Of course everything's in order," she said, her thick arms crossed tightly over her housecoat, closing the matter.

"It was my responsibility. I'd prefer to check."

"If you must," she said in a resigned voice, then brought him the keys.

If she would only confess and face up to it, he would see her through the ordeal ahead. He must attempt to lead her to confess, even though odds were high she wouldn't. "How do you feel about John's death?"

"Distressed. I believe we'll lose guests over it."

He shouldn't be shocked by her emotionless response, but he was. Had she no remorse at all?

"I doubt that," he said.

"Guests don't like seamy business. This has been seamy."

He decided to be completely direct. "Were you with John at the overlook?"

"Of course not!" she screeched. "That little idiot's got you believing her."

"Settle down."

"I won't be accused."

"Calm down."

"I detest that little snip."

"You can't live with hate. It'll eat you up."

She laughed shrilly. "I can and it doesn't."

Repelled, Mark stepped back. He couldn't find any of the love he believed he must have for her.

Furious now, she spat, "Don't step back from me, little brother. You're the one that's off base. You're the one who's siding with Anne."

Fearing she might harass Anne, Mark said, "I don't want you making Anne's work here difficult."

Emma's face puckered into a sour expression. She had no intention of following his advice.

"I mean it," he said firmly. "You will treat her with consideration. I *will not* permit otherwise."

14

After dinner Madeline disappeared without a word as to her destination, and Anne was alone in the room. Alice Gilbert, the third-floor maid, had the room beside Anne's, and Anne figured she had been swimming and had gotten water in her ears again, because her television set blared. Anne's thoughts weren't so much on the noise as on the way Mark's eyes had followed her in the dining room. Or had they? Was it only that she was so in love with him that she had imagined his attention? She couldn't stand thinking that; rather, she would concentrate on looking her best for tonight. She put on her slimming short navy skirt, delicate white blouse, and gold chain with the small gold cross, a gift from her father.

When Mark called for her, he whistled softly. Anne's cheeks flushed. Sure now he was attracted to her, she found it difficult to concentrate on the business at hand as they searched John's car, room, the cartons of his possessions that Emma had stacked in his closet. Mark told Anne about the conversation in Emma's room, and his conclusion that Emma was responsible for John's death. *What a relief to have his full support!* Anne thought. Their search turned up no evidence, which didn't surprise them. Mark suggested that tomorrow evening they try to find testimony which would establish motive or intent. "We need to question people as soon as possible before their memories dim."

They then walked to the beach fronting the Rosses' cottage and sat on a log. Mark was concerned for Anne's skirt.

"It doesn't matter. It's washable."

The Rosses' cottage was boarded and sat like a black box behind them. The stars were on the pines and the June air as soft as cat's fur. No one was on the small beach. Probably the nearest person was half a mile away. Struck by their isolation, by the feel of his strong arm against hers, Anne felt as light as the air around her.

She looked up at Mark's dark, angled face. He grinned and her heart stalled. "You look pretty in this starlight," he said.

The way she felt made her glad she was sitting.

Mark turned her face toward his. "*Very pretty.*"

Their lips were close, but she couldn't allow a kiss. She didn't want her emotions completely carried away. They already had a head start on her. She also knew what her father would think of the situation.

But while her mind went in that direction, her emotions must have gone in another. Because she didn't draw back. His kiss was tender and all she had dreamed it would be. Her head spun, and only with great effort did she manage to release herself from his embrace.

"I shouldn't be doing this," she ventured.

"Why not?" he said lightly, evidently not believing she was serious.

"Because you don't have the same convictions as I do."

His voice was defensive. "I'm a grown man. I can't be governed by old-fashioned rules."

Tears spilled down her cheeks, as she said without thinking, "Maybe we're too different then."

Mark looked long at her. She was sure he was viewing their differences, seeing the impossibility of their relationship. She was surprised when he gently wiped her tears. Shouldn't he be drawing away?

"Forgive me for being so harsh," he said.

She nodded. She didn't trust her voice.

"We can overcome our differences," he said.

"But, how?"

"We just won't do anything that interferes with your Christian principles." It sounded so simple when he put it that way.

Anne was overwhelmed. He actually wanted to continue seeing her.

He pulled her to her feet. "I respect you for wanting to do what you feel is right."

Anne felt a little uneasy. If she fully held to her convictions, she wouldn't even be dating Mark. But he said he wouldn't compromise her Christian beliefs, and that was sufficient. Wasn't it?

After Anne left Mark, she went to her room and got ready for bed. Madeline was still out. Anne had last seen her strolling down the boardwalk with Rick Hobert, her head turned attentively to him. An odd pair, Anne had thought. Madeline had waved vaguely at her and Mark, hardly seeming to notice them. But Anne was sure she must have noticed and been at least slightly upset. Anne was still concerned about hurting Madeline.

She needn't have worried.

When Madeline burst into the room close to midnight, she buzzed around like a bee that had found a good flower. "Rick's quite fascinating," she chirped.

Anne was surprised to hear that. She couldn't imagine anyone less likely to appear fascinating to the flamboyant Madeline.

"Of course those thick-lens glasses of his have got to go," Madeline declared. "They make his eyes look like grapefruits."

Anne was still trying to catch up with her surprise.

Madeline put on her slippers and leaned against the dresser. "He's *got* to get contacts. He says he won't. He says he's afraid to put his finger near his eye—which is a totally ridiculous fear. I've suggested he see a psychiatrist. I will *not* date a man who wears glasses."

Anne laughed.

"Don't laugh. I'm serious—it's either contacts or me. By the way, what's your opinion of him?"

"I like him. He and I are pretty good friends."

"He's rich," Madeline continued happily. "Extremely rich. His father's paint company is the second largest in the country. Although Rick and I didn't discuss the subject, I assume Rick'll be president when his father retires."

Upset with Madeline's line, Anne said, "It sounds like you're more fond of his potential than you are of him."

"Of course not. You've forgotten I never like a man's money unless I first like him."

Anne frowned, crawled into bed, and propped her pillows behind her. When it came to money and men, she and Madeline would never agree. "You'll be careful with Rick, won't you? He's kind of vulnerable. He could be easily hurt."

"Of course—I'm not a femme fatale, you know," she said indignantly.

Oh, really? Anne thought. She had thought it a good description of her.

Anne expressed another worry. "Did it bother you to see me with Mark tonight?"

"Of course. Nobody likes rejection."

"I'm sorry."

"Don't be. If I were you, I wouldn't even have asked."

When the light was out, and Anne was comfortably curled up with one of her pillows in her arms, Madeline said, "Did you know Rick's religious?"

Anne was surprised that Madeline, an atheist, would mention it. "Yes, I guess he is—he's a Christian, you know."

"I didn't ask for a definition. I don't understand the

picky distinctions you Christians make between religions."

Madeline's bed creaked as she turned. "Good-night," she told Anne, ending a discussion she apparently wished she hadn't brought up.

15

$\mathcal{B}$y Saturday, Rick had his contact lenses, Hazel had been hired as Reverend Lindsey's live-in housekeeper, and Weedy Clark had almost stopped berating himself for not anticipating John's death.

And Tessie had a new poem to tack above the buffet:
"When you look below and see the pie,
Take heed you don't just pass it by.
When your hand prepares to rake the cake . . ."

Anne lowered the paper and asked Tessie, "What does 'rake the cake' mean?"

Anne had just finished working breakfast and Tessie was at her worktable, starting her baking. "It means that kids shouldn't put their fingers in the icing. Can't you tell that?"

"No," Anne said, laughing.

Tessie took the paper and sighed. "Then I'll work on it some more tonight."

Tessie's eyes brightened. "Why didn't you tell me?"

"About what?"

"That you and Mark were dating."

"Oh, well—because we just started."

Tessie picked up her wooden spoon. "From now on you tell me." She shook the spoon at her. "You know what things I want to know."

Smiling, Anne left. The last three evenings she and Mark had been searching for testimony, asking questions of a good number of the staff, guests, and deliverymen. They had turned up no evidence. Today they would continue their search. At no time during the last few days had Mark said anything about how much he cared for her. Why not? Surely he was very fond of her—wasn't he?

She changed from her uniform to jeans and met Mark on the veranda. "We'll question Mom today," he said. "She's coming as soon as she gets her pies in the oven."

A moment later Tessie dashed in, flopped into a squeaky rocker, and sipped from her glass of iced tea. Before Mark and Anne could get to their business, Tessie was discussing Alfred, the new handyman. "He's got arthritis, but he gets his work done. He's what you'd call slow, but sure. You can't expect miracles out of anybody anymore. And he did get started on the stairs to the beach. Did you notice?"

"I noticed," said Mark. *Everyone* had noticed, and had been making terse comments about the yellow steps and red railing.

Mark steered Tessie from Alfred to Emma. "Did you think Emma was very upset about John's death, Mom?"

"Why should she be?"

"I'd heard she was quite fond of him."

Tessie's eyes widened in surprise. "*Emma* fond of John? Impossible. She hasn't looked at a man in years."

"Since when?"

"College days. She dated one of her professors for several months, then broke it off. She never said why. She's not one to discuss her personal life . . . not even with her mother," Tessie said regretfully.

Seeing Tessie had no testimony of worth, Mark leaned over and kissed her forehead. "We'd better let you get back to work."

———

By midafternoon Anne and Mark had only two people

left to question: Judy Dixon, the second-floor maid, and Alice Gilbert, the third-floor maid. So far, they had unearthed no useful testimony, and Anne was feeling discouraged.

They found Judy Dixon in room 206, bent over her vacuum. Mark touched her arm and the bony woman leaped to attention, jolting her uniform above her knobby knees. Judy yanked down her skirt and pulled the vacuum wand from under the bed. "You almost took me out'a my socks," she squeaked.

"Sorry, I didn't mean to frighten you," Mark said.

"If you would, sir, you might find it better to knock."

Mark nodded. The room smelled like burning rubber and he said, "Your vacuum needs a new belt."

"I know, sir, but I always hate to request a new part when the old one's got some working left in it. Besides, Miss McGill gets upset if we replace parts before it's absolutely necessary. And she being the boss and all . . ."

Mark nodded his understanding, then asked before she could finish, "Did you know John Blake very well?"

"Bless his soul," she said, crossing her chest to show her respect. But the sorrow didn't go deep, for she dropped her hand and said with distaste, "It ain't right to down-talk the dead, but . . ." For five minutes she maligned John—his drinking, his inability to get his work done, his looseness with women. "He was a no good no-good," she concluded.

"Did he ever date any of the staff, that you know of?"

"Not me!" she said indignantly.

Judy lowered her voice to indicate something of interest was coming. "I shouldn't be telling you this, because you know I ain't a gossip like Alice Gilbert. John had himself a girl friend from here. When I saw him with her, I almost had myself a heart attack. They were slipping up the steps to his room in the dark—real fast like, so no one would know who they was."

"*Who* was the woman?" Mark asked impatiently.

"Miss McGill," she said matter-of-factly.

"Did you happen to overhear anything they said?" he asked.

"No, but I saw them all right, and with my own eyes."

"Did you see them alone together at any other time?"

"No, but I *know* what I saw, and with my own eyes," she emphasized again.

They left Judy to finish her work, pleased to have testimony to corroborate Anne's assertion that Emma and John were romantically involved, but frustrated that they still had no evidence to directly establish motive or intent.

"What if Alice doesn't have any testimony? Then what's our next step?" Anne asked.

"I don't know. We'll have to think about that when the time comes."

They headed for the third floor and Alice Gilbert. But before they could knock on her door the maid filling in for her appeared to say that Alice was in bed with the flu. Because Alice was a television addict, she relished her illnesses, using them as opportunities to catch up on her game shows and soaps. Chances were she would be laid up until next weekend.

"I hate to wait!" Anne exclaimed.

"We've got no choice."

"But you'll be thinking of other possibilities?"

"I will."

Mark then walked Anne to the door of her room. Alice's TV was on low, and they could hear the faint voice of a game-show host. No one was in the ell and Mark took Anne into his arms. "I really like you a lot, Anne," he said.

Finally, he was almost telling her he loved her, and her joy made her whisper, "I like you, too."

"I've been giving our relationship some thought; I think there are problems."

"Problems?" Confused, she wondered how there could be any problems when everything seemed to be going so well.

"Your Christianity. I can't take it lightly. I am *not* a Christian, I am *not* studying to be a missionary—spiritually we're a hundred and eighty degrees apart."

Though she knew he wasn't a Christian, it shocked her to hear him state it outright. She loved him, and couldn't bear to end their relationship so abruptly. "We're really not so far apart in our beliefs."

"I don't want you proselytizing me, Anne. I accept you as you are and I want you to accept me as I am. Can you?"

It would be difficult to tell him she would never attempt to lead him to Christ. *Oh, Lord*, she thought, *please help me say the right thing*. "I won't force my Christianity on you, and I do accept you as you are."

"Sounds good to me," he smiled.

He bent and kissed her lips gently for just a moment, just long enough for Anne to put aside her fears and concentrate on their wonderful future.

16

*W*hile Anne changed into her uniform, she was distraught, and though Madeline was talking animatedly, Anne heard just snatches of her conversation: Rick and she went to Reily after lunch. Rick got a lash under his contact and his eye watered like a hose. Anne's mind was on the conversation she had had with Mark several minutes ago. Her guilt over it forced her to face 2 Corinthians 6:14–15, Scripture she had memorized years ago: "Do not be yoked together with unbelievers. For what do righteousness and wickedness have in common? Or what fellowship can light have with darkness? What harmony is there between Christ and Belial [Satan]? What does a believer have in common with an unbeliever?"

According to the Word, what fellowship could she have with Mark, an unbeliever?

None—none at all.

Anne started to cry. "What's wrong?" Madeline said in an amazed tone. "What can possibly be depressing about Rick's mother's half-carat diamond pendant?"

"It's—I can't talk about it."

"Talk about it!" she demanded in her usual direct manner.

"It's Mark."

Madeline drove on. "What about him?"

"He's not a Christian. My dad wouldn't want me to be dating him."

"Your dad's narrow."

"It's not just Dad. It's God." Anne's tears flowed freely.

"Then He's narrow too!" Madeline exclaimed.

Anne shook her head. *Of course Madeline wouldn't understand,* she thought. *I'm a fool to be discussing this with her.*

Madeline continued, "My advice is to forget all your Bible school theories and enjoy your summer with Mark. You've got a boyfriend you really like—so enjoy him!"

"They aren't theories, Madeline."

"Humph," was her reply as she handed Anne a tissue.

Anne dried her eyes and Madeline nodded approvingly as she saw the tears stop. *Maybe she's right,* Anne thought, determining to stop worrying and enjoy her summer.

———————

Because Mark had a business dinner in Hart on Saturday evening and a lot of work to catch up on Sunday, he wasn't free to see Anne until Sunday after dinner.

On Sunday afternoon Anne changed into a red one-piece swimsuit and joined Madeline on the beach. Madeline had the day off and had been on the beach since noon. She brought a beach umbrella, but lay beside it, preferring to use it as a shelter for her suntan lotion, radio, purse, towel, sunglasses, thongs, books, and beach robe. She lay in the shade of the boathouse where the sun wouldn't dry out her skin completely. The radio was tuned in to her favorite program, *Classics Theater.*

"How's the play?" Anne said as she lay down on her towel.

"Sh-h," she admonished. "It's at the exciting part."

Anne closed her eyes and let the sun make red patterns behind her lids. When *Romeo and Juliet* was finished, Madeline said emphatically, "Someday Madeline Radcliff will be as famous as Shakespeare."

Anne grinned, believing that if it were possible for anyone to become that famous, it would be Madeline.

Madeline twirled the radio dial, and finding nothing but talk shows and country music she turned it off. "I've decided what Rick needs."

"What?"

"A deus ex machina."

"What's that?"

"In Greek drama it was the god who hung over the stage on a crane. He dropped down and intervened in hopeless situations."

"Is Rick in a hopeless situation?"

"He's ill and his thinking's gone haywire—"

Shocked, Anne broke in, "Terminally?" Though Rick was too thin, he had appeared healthy enough when she had seen him yesterday.

Madeline sat up and said impatiently, "If you would please hear me out, you wouldn't jump to such preposterous conclusions. Rick's got the flu—what's hopeless is his attitude. He says he isn't the tycoon type. He says he isn't a leader of men. What I'm getting at is, he refuses to consider running his dad's company. He insists he only wants to be a chemist in one of his dad's labs."

"What's hopeless about that?"

She glared at Anne. "Good grief, you're as dense as he is. Don't you see he's throwing away what could be a brilliant future? I won't let him do it."

"Why do you care about his future?"

"Because I might be part of it."

"Then you're serious about him?"

"Of course—that's what I was just saying."

"That still doesn't give you the right to tell him how to lead his life."

"He needs my guidance, and he'll get it," she declared.

Madeline stood, folded her umbrella, and began packing her things into a canvas beach bag. "As a matter of fact,

I'm going to talk to him again now."

Despite the heavy bag hanging from her shoulder and the awkward umbrella under her arm, she walked gracefully away to seek her conquest.

Troubled, Anne hoped that Rick would somehow withstand.

———

Mark worked all day Sunday, and in the late afternoon he became so absorbed in a brief that he didn't glance at his watch until 7:30. He had worked longer than he intended, but then, he usually did. He put in a 60–80 hour week and he would do so from now until the day he had the largest law practice in the county. He would be calling for Anne at 8:30, but before that he needed dinner. He closed his folder and drove to Richard's, a small truck stop on the outskirts of Reily, which served the best chili in the area.

He ordered the Sunday special, a large bowl of chili sprinkled with cheese, and assorted crackers on the side. When the chili came, Mark stirred in a handful of crushed crackers and ate absently, his mind on Anne. Lately when he wasn't absorbed with work, his thoughts were on her and her religion. Their religious views were opposite, yet Anne said this didn't bother her. But how could that be, when her Christianity wasn't just an idle philosophy but a course of study and a life pursuit?

Richard, who sometimes served as well as cooked, interrupted his thoughts. "More coffee?"

Mark pushed his cup toward the tipped pot, and after Richard filled it, he considered Anne's Christianity from another angle. Could it be he found her attractive because of it? Maybe. But if so, it was just one of her many qualities he admired.

The thought perplexed him and he set down his spoon. Did he love Anne? How could he, when he'd only been dating her for a few days? On the other hand, he had known her for two years. He had always been fond of her, though in a brotherly way. Maybe their long association had provided a basis for love. And maybe a time or two he had felt more than brotherly affection, but had suppressed his feelings because of her age.

His analysis ended abruptly and a soft feeling of love for Anne overcame him, a feeling that he would like to hold her and care for her forever. Did she love him? He sensed she did, but he wouldn't rest until he heard the admission from her.

———

When Anne left the beach, she changed into her uniform and found Madeline in the kitchen, ladling out a large bowl of chicken broth for Rick, expressing concern because his temperature was 101 degrees and he was splayed out in bed like a broken branch. To Anne's relief, Madeline hadn't bugged Rick about being a tycoon. Madeline was too busy nursing him, a task which she evidently enjoyed, for she marched off purposely with the soup. Anne smiled, thinking Madeline certainly was an all-right person at times.

Pam, the waitress filling in for Madeline, wandered into the kitchen and Anne led her to the dining room. This was Pam's first night and Anne tried to train her, a seemingly impossible task. She was a slow-moving and slow-thinking young woman and most of Anne's directions seemed to float right through her blond head. By 6:30 Pam had asked twice where the mustard was, three times where the sugar was, and why the silverware drawer was in the dining room, not in the kitchen. "We need the silverware by the tables," Anne explained.

Because Pam was dragging around in a daze, Anne was doing most of Pam's work as well as all of her own; therefore she was especially irritated when Emma raised her hand for the third time. During meals Emma read bird books and motioned to the waitresses when she needed seconds or thirds on food. All of the guests, except the Comptons who were quite old, served themselves, and Anne resented the extraordinary service Emma demanded. Anne hurried to her table, and Emma said crisply over her bird book, "A roll and two pats of butter."

Anne brought a hard roll, a croissant, and two pats of butter.

"I asked for one roll," Emma said, taking the croissant from the basket.

"You didn't say which kind you wanted, so I brought you a choice."

"If I had wanted a choice I'd have so indicated," she snapped.

Anne forced herself not to frown, but she couldn't stop the irritated note in her response. "Okay, next time I'll know."

"Don't be short with me, young lady." Emma laid down the book and motioned for Anne to move nearer. "Mother mentioned that she told you about the professor I dated in college. That's private business. Don't let it pass your lips."

"Well, of course not—but I certainly couldn't have helped hearing what your mother shared."

"Don't make excuses," she said gruffly. "My past is my affair and I prefer to keep it that way."

Anne was getting angry.

"Be *sure* you keep it to yourself," Emma commanded and snapped off the tip of her croissant.

"Yes, ma'am," Anne said and left her. *Take it easy*, she thought. *You expected her to give you a hard time this summer, so just accept her.* Odd though, she felt more than an air of hard times to come following her across the dining room; she felt hate, like a black breeze on her back.

Because Pam was slow, it took longer than usual to

clean up the dining room. Anne was going crazy. She doubted she'd have time to bathe and dress in time to meet Mark.

Just as she was leaving for her room, Anne stopped short in the front hall. Rick was wobbling in front of a couch, and Madeline was grasping his shoulders. Suddenly she released him and his long, slight body floated onto the couch. Some soda from the can he held splattered his slacks, and he wiped them with the arm of his shirt. He raised his shoulders slightly, then immediately collapsed.

Madeline's call was urgent. "Please, come quickly, Anne."

"I'm late, Madeline."

"I *need* you."

Anne went dutifully. "Look at him," Madeline scowled. "I left him in his room, and fifteen minutes later I found him at the soda machine, sticking fifty cents in a slot. He doesn't belong out of bed. He's practically dead, but he insists he needs a break from his bed. Have you ever heard of anything so ridiculous?"

Rick raised his pale face and said weakly, "If I want a break I think I should take one."

"Tell him he's wrong," Madeline insisted. "He won't listen to me."

"You really should stay in bed," Anne said, thoroughly agreeing with Madeline. "You could have called one of us to bring you a drink."

Rick coughed and when he was able to speak there was a little spirit in his voice, "If *you* were in my bed, you'd have left it too."

"Why on earth do you say that?" Madeline demanded.

"Because of Weedy. He's playing again." Weedy roomed with Rick and had recently taken up the harmonica. He mouthed it uncertainly and pulled out so many flat notes that even he wasn't sure what song he played.

"Why didn't you tell him to quit?" asked Madeline.

"I did, but he didn't hear me. He was too absorbed in his music."

"Well, he won't be for long," Madeline said, pulling Rick up from the couch. "I'm having a talk with him."

"I can do my own talking," Rick said as Madeline led him away.

17

$\mathcal{B}$ecause of Rick and his break from bed, Anne was left with just two minutes to dress, so she phoned Mark and delayed their date a half hour. She sank into a scented bath, then put on a red dress that complimented her cute figure. She had just fastened the last button when Mark knocked. Mark's eyes confirmed his approval. He reached for her hand, and as they walked toward the staircase, he said, "I'd like to talk to you in private. My room—" He broke off. "No, let's make it Rosses' beach."

She sensed it was about their relationship, not their investigation. When they came to the veranda, they were met by thunder and ribs of lightning. The walk was out, so Mark led Anne to the dining room, seating her at a table for two back by the buffet, where they would have the most privacy.

After meals, coffee and hot water for tea were available for the guests and staff. Mark brought them coffee, then lit their candle, a short stick in a wax-covered bottle.

Anne added sugar and cream to her coffee and, impatient to hear his news, said, "You had something to tell me."

"Yes, about us. I—"

"Hi," someone hollered.

Anne turned to see Weedy Clark bustling over. She hoped he would be quick; fortunately he usually was. He pulled up a chair, set his harmonica on the table, and groaned. "I've been kicked out of my room. Madeline thinks my harmonica playing is killing Rick."

"He *is* sick," Anne said.

"He should've told me to stop, then."

"He did, but you didn't hear him."

"Well, he shouldn't have dragged Madeline up. She had no right to blast at me."

Mark's eyes focused suddenly. He hadn't been listening. "Hmm," he said.

With imperfect timing, Madeline swept into the dining room and over to the table. Mark brought her a chair and offered her a cup of coffee. Though she loved coffee, she refused. Earlier Madeline had told Anne she was giving up coffee because she had read in *Sophisticated Woman* that its impurities caused premature wrinkles.

Madeline gave Mark and Weedy cool looks. Weedy scowled at Madeline. Mark looked distracted. Anne's face was passive, but she was filled with impatience. If only Madeline and Weedy would leave so she and Mark could have their talk!

"Rick's resting quietly," said Madeline. "His fever broke a half hour ago."

"That's great," said Anne.

Mark nodded.

"And what do you have to say?" Madeline asked Weedy in a nasty tone.

"He wasn't that sick."

The conversation hobbled along until the desk clerk brought news that Mark had an urgent phone call. When he returned, he explained he had to leave for the police station; a man just arrested for assault and battery requested that Mark represent him.

Anne walked Mark to his car, where he put his arms around her and told her he would be at a trial in Grand Rapids on Monday and Tuesday. "I won't be back until Wednesday," he said. His voice was troubled. "I don't like to keep you hanging, but I can't rush through what I've got to say now."

"I guess it'll have to wait," Anne said resignedly.

He smiled, pleased that she so readily understood. He had never met such an unselfish a girl.

She watched his green Ford travel down the lane until the car blended into the forest; then she reluctantly returned to the inn.

———

By Tuesday, Anne's spirits were low, Rick reported for work, and Alice Gilbert was thinking about returning to work. "I saw her peekin' into the hall," said Judy Dixon.

Tuesday after dinner, Weedy called Anne to the front desk and said, "How about a date tonight, barefoot?"

"No . . . I'm going to Tessie's." Fortunately, Tessie had invited Anne to tea.

He ignored that and leaned across the counter, placing his face inches from Anne's. His medium brown eyes brightened with far more longing than she believed he felt. "I'm off in thirty minutes. Call off your date with Tessie and go to town with me."

"She's expecting me."

"You *always* refuse me."

"Well—" Anne said, hoping he would understand that meant he should stop asking.

Understanding came into his eyes. "Is Mark the reason you won't go?"

"No, I said I was going to see Tessie."

"Do you like Mark?"

"Yes, of course."

"Then I suppose I'll have to wait my turn."

"Oh, Weedy!" Anne said, shaking her head but smiling.

A couple arrived to check in and Weedy hurried off saying, "Keep me posted."

Tessie lived in a suite of rooms behind the kitchen. She ushered Anne into her hyper-hued living room, where orange satin pillows jangled against a green couch, and cream draperies hung on yellow walls. Tessie served tea and brownies, kicked off her slippers, and curled up in a blue chair. Though she smiled bravely, her eyes filled with tears. "I just can't keep it to myself. Sometimes . . . Emma . . . I . . . ." She collapsed in tears.

While Anne worried over what Tessie's problem might be, Tessie gulped at her tea and gathered herself together. Finally she was able to explain. "This morning Emma charged Mr. Barnes fifty dollars too much, and you know how exacting he is. He got upset, but instead of apologizing, she told him we could do without cranks like him. Mr. Barnes said he'd never be back and his face turned as purple as that." Tessie pointed to the ceramic pot beside her chair that held a spindly, dying schefflera.

Tessie's tears flowed again. "I told Emma to apologize to Mr. Barnes and she screamed at me—her own mother! Screamed—right in my face!"

"I'm sorry," Anne consoled, despising Emma.

"She's never done that before. What's wrong with her?"

"I don't know." But Anne really wondered if Emma was edgy because of the guilt she must feel over John's death.

Tessie gave a sigh that rocked her round frame and answered her own question. "It's her past catching up with her," Tessie explained. "When Emma was a year old, I contracted tuberculosis and subsequently spent four years in a sanatorium. At that time Emma was the only child. During those years, she lived with Jim's Aunt Ursula, a woman so distraught that no one would even sit beside her at the monthly meeting of her garden club. I think Emma picked up her ways." Tessie shook her head sadly.

"I'm sorry. I didn't know."

"It's not just Aunt Ursula, it's heredity. Her great-grandmother was a horror. But a mother always hopes her child will be different. A mother always prays."

Anne felt guilty. She hadn't prayed for Miss McGill. In fact, she hadn't even thought of doing so, nor did she feel like doing so now. How could she feel like it, when Miss McGill had been responsible for a man's death? when Miss McGill hated her? when frankly, she just plain didn't like her? Yet according to God, she should forgive Miss McGill, should love her and pray for her.

But Anne couldn't.

Relieved, now that her burden was shared, Tessie offered Anne another brownie and asked, "Do you love my Mark?"

Anne was taken aback and blushed. "Of course not, Tessie. Not yet. We're just dating." She couldn't admit her feelings. Tessie would fly off the handle with happiness, have no constraint, tell everyone. That would be awful!

Noting the blush, Tessie smiled and said slyly, "Really?"

"Yes, really," Anne said firmly.

———

Wednesday evening when the sun was down and the sky lavender-gray, Anne held Mark's hand and dug her running shoes into the side of a steep dune. A hundred feet below them the forest met the dune. They were headed for a small pond at the base, and before Anne saw it, she heard the frogs and the rustle of stiff marsh grass. They edged down to the pond, and Mark laid out a plaid car blanket. A cool breeze started up, and after Anne had sat down, she buttoned her cardigan to the top. Several frogs croaked in chorus, a sound that agitated her. She realized she was too excited, but she couldn't contain herself. She had waited three days for this talk. Was Mark about to tell her he loved her? What if he didn't? She couldn't bear the suspense any longer.

Mark placed his arm around her shoulder and said,

"You've never talked much about your missionary plans. Are you very set on being one?"

How could she answer that? If he loved her, she wouldn't leave Reily. If he didn't, she would. "Kind of."

"Where will you go?"

"Probably New Guinea."

"In a few years you'll be thousands of miles from me."

"Not necessarily," she said. "I might not go."

"What would change your mind?"

"Circumstances." *Please make your point,* Anne thought, *before I go crazy!*

"What kind of circumstances?"

Anne answered as straightforwardly as she could. "If the man I loved had other plans, I might not go."

Mark gave a mental sigh of relief at Anne's answers. Thank heaven, she wasn't so set on doing missionary work, after all. If she had been, he couldn't have offered her the ring. While in Grand Rapids, he had bought her an engagement ring—an emerald-cut diamond set in a plain band of gold. It was an impulsive act, generated by his ardent love for Anne and by a strong feeling that she would accept the ring. At that time he hadn't considered Anne's career plans. While walking to the dunes, he had. If Anne were set on doing missionary work, how could they marry? He had his career, his plans for success. He couldn't give them up to follow her to the mission field.

He moved his hand, about to take the ring from his pocket, then released it, his mind throwing up a fresh set of doubts. He was determined to be successful. Would Anne be the right type of wife for him? Facing her would be business-related affairs important to his career: dinners with clients, cocktail parties. How would unworldly Anne, who didn't even drink, fit into that environment? It was important that Anne learn to drink a glass of wine, be a woman with social graces.

Anne laid her head on his shoulder. It seemed so right that she should be there. His doubts left. She would adjust to his life as perfectly as she adjusted to work at the inn. She was young, teachable, and he would help her learn.

Mark lowered his hand from Anne's shoulder, reached into the pocket of his flannel shirt, and took out the small white box. Anne's breath caught, her eyes fixed on the box. What gift could he be giving her?

Mark opened the lid. An exquisite ring lay on the black velvet cloth, the diamond sparkling in the last gray light of the day.

Mark's eyes were set on hers, shadows accentuating his rugged face. "Anne, will you marry me?" he asked simply. He raised his hand to halt her answer. "Please understand, if you need time to think it over, I'm willing to wait."

She had hoped for love, but her wildest imagination couldn't have produced a proposal so soon. Stunned, she could only manage a whisper. "I do want to marry you, Mark."

He took her hand gently, and slipped the ring on her finger. "I love you," he said, and kissed her as if she were the only girl he had ever cared for.

Time and space merged for Anne, and she felt lifted to a very high place, where there was only love and joy and happiness forever.

"I love you so much," Anne said, "I can hardly think of anything else. I never dreamed this could happen so fast."

"Anne, I'd like to be the one to tell your dad about our engagement."

Anne came down to earth. *Of all times to be reminded of Dad!* she thought in despair. Dad was so strong about a Christian marrying a Christian. She could just imagine how Mark's talk with her father would go. No, she must speak to Dad before Mark did. She must have Dad's promise that he would congratulate Mark, bless their plans.

Mark drew her from her reverie. "Why the silence?"

"Let me tell Dad," she said, forcing her voice not to show her concern.

"But, Anne," he said firmly, "I should have asked your father for your hand. Since I didn't, I'd like to be the one to announce our plans."

"But, you can't, Mark. I mean, he may not understand."

"Don't be silly," he said in an incredulous tone.

"I've got to, Mark. Please let me," she pleaded.

"Why?"

"I just want to."

"Anne, this is important to me. Please, let's do this my way," he insisted.

"All right," she conceded. But her mind raced with how she could get to her dad first with the news.

"He's out tonight," she guessed. "Don't call him until tomorrow."

He nodded, then said, "Okay, but let's not tell anyone we're engaged until I talk to your dad. He should be the first to know."

"Fine. I'm sure that's right." Anne tried to sound agreeable.

Anne was depressed. *How ridiculous!* she thought. This should be the happiest day of her life, and she was feeling depressed! Somehow she would reconcile the Bible and Mark and Dad. There had to be a way.

18

$\mathcal{M}$adeline read in *Sophisticated Woman* that a facial of honey, yogurt, and vinegar would prevent wrinkles. Because she had indulged in five cups of coffee earlier, she mixed up a jar of the facial and was spreading it on when Anne came in from the dunes. "Would you believe I actually found a fine wrinkle line on my forehead?" she said.

"No kidding," Anne said. Her hand was caressing the ring box in her cardigan pocket. If only she could share her news with Madeline. And if only she didn't have to get to Dad with the news in the shortest possible time.

"When I rinse this off I'll show you," Madeline said, frosting her face with the last of the facial.

Madeline settled into the easy chair and muttered, "Rick *still* refuses to consider running his dad's company." She wiped the drippy facial from her lips with a tissue. "I've suggested he take a course in assertiveness. I've explained that it's no stigma to do so. Even I, who am naturally assertive, have taken assertiveness training. But he won't consider it. I want you to talk to him, Anne, and insist he go."

Anne came awake to the conversation. "I think he knows what's best for himself, Madeline."

"Are you or aren't you my friend?"

"I am, but I don't think you should boss him around so much. Men need to have the last say in certain areas."

"All right," she said huffily. "I'll manage him *without* your help."

102

Anne started for the door. To have privacy, she would have to phone Dad from the booth in the front hall. "Where are you going?" Madeline asked.

"I'll be right back."

"That doesn't answer my question."

"To get a soda—or something." Why did Madeline have to know what she was doing every moment of the day!

When Anne reached her father, she could hear voices in the background. "Do you have company, Dad?"

"The elders are here for a meeting."

"Will they leave soon?"

"No—it'll be late."

What bad luck! she thought.

"I really can't talk now, dear," he said. "Was it something important?"

"Well—" She broke off, deciding she couldn't condense her news. She needed far more than a few minutes to break it to him. "I'll call you back later, Dad."

"Honey, if it'll keep, I'd really rather talk to you tomorrow evening. I've got to leave at dawn for a seminar in Muskegon, and I should get to bed right after this meeting."

Anne's mind tried to grasp a quick solution. Dad was leaving early tomorrow and evidently getting home late; if she asked him to stop at the inn after the seminar, there was no way Mark could reach him before she did. She could meet him in the lot and they'd talk in the car. "Why don't you come here after your seminar, Dad? We could talk then."

"You're sure nothing's wrong, Anne?"

"No—no—nothing at all."

"I'll see you about nine, then," he said. "Good-night, dear."

"Good-night, Dad—and Dad, I'll meet you in the parking lot. We need to talk privately." Anne hung up quickly, before he could question her request. The short conversation had drained her, and she wished she didn't have to go through all these secret plans and arrangements. Her last thoughts on the matter before returning to her room were to be in the lot before 9:00 so as to catch him as soon as he arrived. They could drive off together somewhere to be sure Mark didn't see them talking. What made things even more difficult was the fact that she even felt guilty about asking the Lord to help her through the trauma of approaching her dad with the subject.

———

In the morning, Mark phoned Anne from his office with the news that her father's secretary said that he was in Muskegon. Mark hoped to talk to him tomorrow and arrange an appointment. Mark went on to say that Tessie had phoned to chat and had informed him that Alice Gilbert had left her sickbed reluctantly but quickly this morning when Emma threatened to fire her.

"I hope you don't mind, Anne," Mark said; "but I went ahead and phoned Alice and arranged for us to meet her around eight-thirty this evening in the dining room."

Mind? It was impossible! Anne thought wildly, almost overcome by this new problem. Dad would be here about nine. What if the meeting lasted more than half an hour? Surely it would.

"Fine," she said, because she couldn't think of another thing to say. If she had to leave, she'd just leave. She could say her stomach was upset.

———

After dinner Anne and Mark waited for Alice Gilbert in the dining room. Alice was late and Anne nervously glanced at her watch: 8:33. "Where is she?" Anne tried not to sound impatient.

"She walks slowly, remember?" Mark smiled.

"She should've left her room earlier." Anne was on the verge of tears.

"Darling, what's a few minutes? Let's enjoy the extra time together."

"Okay," Anne said, forcing a smile.

"I've decided on the next step in our investigation. I'm going to phone John's brother. John could have shared his relationship with Emma with him."

"Oh, sure," Anne said vaguely.

"I should think you'd be interested."

"I am." She would be—after tonight!

At last Alice came thumping into the dining room, her tent-shaped dress drooping from her mountainous shoulders. Alice was huge and she ordered her dresses from Large Is Lovely, a shop in Detroit that specialized in clothes for women over two hundred pounds. She sank into a chair, her body flowing over the seat.

"Sorry I'm late," Alice blurted, "but Eric (the villain in her soap opera) just got drunk and wrecked Grace's car. It blew up and I had to see if he lived."

Alice could go on forever when she started on her soap operas. "That's nice," Anne said, hoping that would end the summary.

"Did he live?" Mark asked politely.

"I don't know yet. He's under the car," she panted. "He took a breath—but it could've been his last. They didn't show no more tonight."

Fortunately, Mark got right down to the business at hand—at least he tried. Each time he asked Alice to comment on John's romantic life, her puffy lids blinked rapidly as she said, "I really can't say."

Obviously she knew something, but if she didn't speak soon, Anne would have to leave. It was 8:43.

Mark tried to persuade her to talk. "I'm not trying to pry. I've got a legal reason for asking about John's love life."

"Well, I don't know—" her voice trailed off.

"Why is it so difficult to make a simple comment?" Mark was getting impatient.

"Because Miss McGill'll fire me if she hears I said something. She's already down on me," she replied with a pout.

"I can promise you won't be fired for being honest with me. It's important that you tell me what you know."

"Well, okay." Her eyes still blinked as she told him that three weeks ago, during a commercial on the late, late movie, she stepped into the hall for a breath of air. There to her amazement, she saw John and Emma kissing at the head of Emma's stairs. Alice managed to duck back into her room unseen. "You promise I won't be in trouble for saying this?" she whispered.

"I promise," Mark assured her. "Did you hear anything they said?"

"Nope, nothing. Like I said, I ran back into my room."

Alice looked at her watch. "I gotta go." She heaved herself up and left abruptly.

Though it was good to have another witness for Emma and John's romance, it still wasn't enough evidence to convince Sergeant Marcum. But, Anne didn't have time to think about that. It was 8:57; she didn't have a minute to waste.

"I've really got to leave too," she spoke to Mark as she stood.

"Why? What's the rush?"

"I'm—well—I'm not feeling well," she said, running her hand over her forehead and through her hair.

"Why's that? Has this rushed interview upset you?"

"No, no, probably something I ate. I'll be fine after I rest a bit."

"Let me take you to your room," he insisted.

Oh, no! she thought, straining for a reason to get away

from him quickly. "I've got to go by myself, Mark. Really, I'll be fine."

Before she could stop him, he had his arm around her waist and was leading her to the elevator in the front hall. The creaking old machine seemed to take forever to come. It was just a few feet from the door through which her father could appear any second if he hadn't waited in the parking lot. "I'm sorry, Mark, but I really feel awful. I'll call you later," she blurted and ran for the stairway.

She'd run up to the second floor, then take the back stairs to the door to the parking lot. She'd have to hope Dad was not in the process of walking across the veranda—and then hope to get back to her room again before Mark came and inquired about her. Feeling hysteria overtake her, she forced herself to take one step at a time. If she needed an excuse for her absence, she would think up one later. Right now, she must get to the parking lot.

Anne's breath was short when she reached the lot. She scanned the cars. Dad's car wasn't there, thank heavens! For once luck was with her. But she must be careful. Mark might come by and she must hide somewhere. Her eyes settled on the ample old oak beside the lot and she hurried behind it.

She glanced at her watch: 9:10. *Come on, Dad,* she silently entreated. They must have a quick talk, so she could get back to her room as soon as possible.

At 9:15 her father arrived. She ran to his blue sedan and jumped in. "We can't stay, Dad. Let's drive to the dunes— I'll tell you about it when we get there," she said in one breathless run-on sentence.

Her father was 44, a handsome man with the hefty frame of a football player. He wore his flannel shirt, the green and black plaid one she had given him last Christmas. He shifted around to face her, puzzled by her behavior. He was quite serious as he said, "You sound panicky. Can't you tell me now?"

"No—just trust me, Daddy."

To her relief, he shifted gears and drove to the dunes, parking on a little lane in the woods that paralleled them. He switched off the headlights and turned to Anne. "All right, what is it?"

Sitting in the car with her dad had a sobering effect on Anne. Clouds blackened the sky, and though they were just yards from the dunes, Anne couldn't see them through the trees. Suddenly her love for him overcame her fears and she flung herself into his arms, crying out, "Oh, Daddy, it's so awful!"

He stroked her hair. "What is it, kitten?" he said gently.

"I'm afraid I'm going to disappoint you," she sobbed.

"Tell me," he said softly.

"It's Mark McGill." Forcing herself to calm down, Anne wiped her eyes, pulled away from her father's arms, and began, "Mark and I are engaged—and Mark's not a Christian. I know you disapprove, but we love each other and we've got to spend our lives together." There, it was out.

"Honey, you're not thinking straight."

"But, Mark's not an atheist. He believes in God. Someday he'll believe in Jesus."

"You can't be sure of that, Anne."

"If you knew him like I did, you would," she pleaded.

Mr. Lindsey simply quoted 2 Corinthians 6:14–15, the Scripture she had been struggling with. "You can't marry a non-Christian," he said. "You and Mark would never be happy."

"But, we've got our love!"

"That's not enough." He was firm.

"In our case it is!"

"You'll be violating God's law if you marry a non-Christian. I want you to give yourself time to reconsider."

"I can't." Then, crushed by the enormous strain of

standing against her father, God, her own beliefs, Anne sobbed out, "I love Mark."

"Have you prayed about this?"

"Not really."

Her father sighed. "Then I assume if you're not about to listen to God, you're not about to listen to me."

It wasn't a question she could answer.

"All right," he said resignedly, "You have a will of your own. I release you to make your own decision."

He paused, then, "I love you, kitten. I'll pray for you and Mark."

She couldn't make out his features, but if his expression was as tender as his voice, she might have changed her mind. She was glad she couldn't see it. There was still one more difficult admission to make. "Mark doesn't know I talked to you, Dad. I promised him he could tell you first. Please don't tell him we talked."

Her father shook his head. "That's an impossible request."

"But what'll I do?"

"You'll tell him you spoke to me," he replied simply. "And you'd best tell him as soon as you get back."

Her agreement was followed by dread. When Mark heard what she had done and why she had done it, he would probably call off the engagement.

19

The candle on the dining room table where Anne sat flickered romantically and dripped a skirt of wax onto the soda bottle. Anne picked at the wax, something she never did and detested others doing. But she was a wreck. After she had left her father, she had phoned Mark and arranged to meet him here. As she had feared, he had stopped by her room earlier while she was out. "I'll explain—meet me in the dining room."

Why was Mark taking so long? she thought nervously. Their conversation would no doubt be quite traumatic; and if she had to anticipate it much longer, she would lose her nerve and flee.

Moments later he arrived, the sound of his irregular step very clear above the chatter of a table of teenagers.

As soon as he sat down, Anne stammered out her confession, "I've talked . . . to Dad."

Mark frowned. "I explicitly asked you not to, Anne."

"I know. I didn't want to, but I had to."

"Then, why?"

Anne had put a small New Testament in her skirt pocket, hoping a reading of 2 Corinthians 6:14–15 would help Mark understand her motives. She took out the Testament and read the verses. "Dad believes a Christian should only marry a Christian. I had to explain my position to him."

"Why didn't you tell me?"

"I couldn't—I got upset and mixed up."

"What *is* your position on that Scripture? Be honest with me." His voice was insistent.

If she stated her true feelings, perhaps he wouldn't marry her. She must tell one last lie. But her heart broke at the words. "I don't believe it in the same way Dad does. Dad's more of a fundamentalist than I."

Relief crossed his face.

"I'm sorry I went behind your back to Dad," she said.

"Just don't do something like that again, Anne. We have to trust each other."

"You're right, Mark, and I won't."

"Does your father accept our engagement?"

"Yes. He said the decision is mine. But, he loves me still, Mark. And he said he would pray for us."

"Good, I appreciate that, considering his stand." Mark went on to say he still hoped to see her father tomorrow, not to cover the same ground Anne had, but to present himself as a future son-in-law. They then set a date for the wedding. It would be August 15, so that they could have a two-week honeymoon before Anne's school began. She decided she would complete her four years, though she wasn't sure yet what course of study she would pursue. After dinner tomorrow, they would tell Jim and Tessie about their engagement.

"Your mom will go nuts when she hears," Anne said.

———

In her baggy housedress, Hazel Green looked like a little note in a big envelope when she let Mark in for his five o'clock appointment with Dr. Lindsey. "Oh my, oh my, sir, I do say it's good to see you," she squeaked, her adoration for the man who had befriended her overcoming her shyness.

Mark laughed and gathered her in his arms. "Oh my,"

she squeaked again, "You're squeezing me right to death."

He released her, studied her, thought she looked stronger and healthier than she had last week. "How's the arm and leg?" he asked.

"Real good," she said, explaining that she was receiving free therapy from a physical therapist who attended Reverend Lindsey's church. "She says in five or six months I'll be good as new."

He grinned, delighted with the news.

Hazel then took Mark to Reverend Lindsey's study. As he entered, Dr. Lindsey rose from behind an oversized desk and shook Mark's hand, motioning him to a chair in front of the desk. The room was small, crammed with a couch, chair, and desk. Hazel served coffee and warm banana-nut bread spread with cream cheese. As she closed the door behind her, she glanced nervously at several stacks of files in the corner.

"I've promised Hazel I'll get a cabinet and file the papers so she can vacuum that corner. But where'll I put it?"

"It won't take much more room than the folders."

"Maybe you're right."

"I assume then that Hazel is working out well for you."

"Very."

Mark went on to his reason for coming. "I'm looking forward to being a part of your family, Reverend Lindsey."

"I'm pleased to have you, son," he replied warmly. "I've heard good comments around town about your law firm."

Though Mark hadn't planned to discuss religion, the Reverend's warm manner and the study itself with its Bibles and commentaries prompted Mark to say, "I won't stand in the way of Anne's Christianity. In fact, I intend to go to church with her." In a sense he was surprised as he hadn't considered attending her church until now. Mark had little experience with churches and could count on his fingers the times he had been in one. Though he seldom prayed now, he had always prayed before bed as a child. He remembered the peace he had felt then and he said, more to himself than to Reverend Lindsey, "I used to think prayer had some benefit."

"It has great benefit, my son."

"Anne has said that she prays."

"Yes, I know she does."

"She prays about everything, I believe."

"Almost."

"Sometimes her faith touches me."

"You can have her kind of faith."

The comment tugged at him. But he knew Anne's faith came from her Christianity, and he wasn't willing to become a Christian. Christians were utterly dependent on God, as dependent as he had been on his parents when he was a child. No, he cherished his ability to control his fate. "I can manage fine with my own kind of faith."

"Someday, you may find you cannot," Reverend Lindsey countered. "Do you know the scripture, 'For all have sinned and come short of the glory of God'?"

"I've heard it."

"There's a moment in every man's life when he finds himself measured against God's holiness."

"Perhaps, but I don't feel measured in any way."

Reverend Lindsey dropped the subject and spoke of general matters. Mark appreciated that; he didn't care for people who pushed their convictions. When he left, he decided he liked Reverend Lindsey, though he did find him rather narrow. Fortunately, Anne wasn't.

———

As Anne and Mark walked through the corridors toward Jim and Tessie's to announce their engagement, Mark told Anne he had phoned Earnest T. Blake, John's brother from Grand Rapids. After Mark explained that he and Anne were conducting a private investigation, Earnest revealed that he had received a letter from John three weeks ago. In it John had written that he dated Emma, that he thought it amusing that Emma had a tantrum and threatened to do him in each time he went out with another woman. Fortunately Earnest was a collector of everything, but unfortunately he had mislaid the letter among his many things. But he was sure he could find it. If he did so quickly, he would send it certified mail. If not, he would bring it with him when he came to Reily to pick up John's personal effects. "That'll be in about two weeks," Mark said.

Their first real break! Anne thought with excitement. Mark went on to say he had phoned Sergeant Marcum to detail Judy's and Alice's testimonies and describe Earnest's letter. Sergeant Marcum agreed he would reopen the case if the contents of the letter actually did show that Emma intended to harm John. But he doubted they would. Rather it sounded to him as if John were amused and making a joke of it. Anne sensed just the opposite; she believed the letter would indeed establish intent to harm.

At Mark's parents' Anne and Mark sat on the sofa while Tessie pulled tissues from the pocket of her old robe and mopped cold cream from her face. "You should have said you were coming, Mark, so I could have been ready for you. I was getting ready for bed a little early tonight."

"We don't mind," said Mark.

"But I do!"

When Tessie's face was wiped clean, she served iced tea and called Jim in to join them. Tessie looked at them questioningly.

Mark began abruptly, "Anne and I are in love, Mom, Dad. We're going to be married."

Tessie almost dropped her glass as she sprang from her chair. "I always knew it!" she said excitedly. "A mother knows and I've always known."

Tessie clasped Anne tightly in her arms and with tears in her eyes said, "I love you, dear. Just think, you'll be my daughter now!"

Anne cried too as she whispered, "Mother." It felt good to say that word again.

Jim gave Anne a quick hug. "I'm pleased," he said softly. Jim seldom said much, but the quiet joy in his eyes spoke volumes.

"When?" Tessie's eyes danced. "I hope it won't be long."

"August fifteenth," Anne announced.

"Wonderful!" Tessie threw her hands in the air.

Tessie loved parties and within minutes she was planning an engagement party for Saturday night, a week from tomorrow. "We'll have the staff, the family, Reverend Lindsey, my friends, all of your friends"—she waved at Anne and Mark—"the delivery people—"

Jim interrupted forcefully. "Not the delivery people. You *do not* have to invite everyone you've ever met to this party."

"But I can't leave anyone out," Tessie insisted, taking out a piece of paper to begin the list. But she was too excited to concentrate on names, and she dropped her pencil and began planning the cake she would serve. "I'll make it myself. It'll have three tiers, red hearts, and red roses—with white icing and—"

Tessie couldn't even concentrate on the cake. "We'll have a pre-celebration tonight," she said. She mixed another pitcher of iced tea and served chocolate mousse pie topped with whipped cream and a cherry. Anne normally counted calories, but tonight really was a celebration and she decided to enjoy it.

The excitement and joy were a bit dampened when Emma stopped in, fresh from the Friday night meeting of the Reily Birdwatcher's Society. She was in a nasty mood, her eyes as mean as the eyes of the silver hawk on the lapel of her suit jacket. "The club refuses to picket the insecticide factory," Emma snapped.

"Are the insecticides killing many of the birds?" asked Tessie.

"Some—but it's not a matter of numbers. No bird should be poisoned."

"Then—"

Emma interrupted her mother. "I came to discuss business, not birds." Emma sat, adjusted the legs of her slacks so the creases cut straight down the center, and continued brusquely. "I realize the dining room's your province," she told Tessie, "but I feel compelled to step in. Pam must be fired. She filled in tonight for Madeline and it took her ten minutes to bring me a side dish of carrots."

"I know she isn't fast," Tessie murmured sadly, "but I can't let her go."

"Why?"

"She might lose confidence in herself. She'll be slower than she is if she doesn't have her confidence."

"Dad," Emma appealed, "tell Mom we run an inn not a clinic."

"Emma's right. You'll have to let her go."

"But Jim! I can't fire anybody, you know that." Tessie's glass quivered in her hand.

Jim softened, as he always did when these kinds of things distressed Tessie. "I'll fire Pam."

Tessie was able to recover her good spirits, and she announced to Emma, "Mark and Anne are engaged."

Emma's face went milk-white, and she flashed Anne a look that chilled Anne through and through. Between lips that didn't move, she uttered, "How nice."

Inexplicably, the look threw Anne's mind into the future. She thought, *If our investigation is successful and Miss McGill is arrested for her part in John's death, I'll look back on this cold moment and think it warm in comparison.* Anne shuddered, imagining how stricken Tessie would be, how Emma would be filled with an anger too terrible to imagine. Yet she sensed they were heading irrevocably for that day.

Anne couldn't take her eyes from Tessie.

"Let me offer my congratulations," Emma told Mark flatly.

"You must have some pie," Tessie told Emma.

"No, I believe I'll skip it. I've got a few matters to attend to," she said and left.

Later, while Mark and Anne were headed for Anne's door, Anne stated, "I wish I'd never seen Emma at the overlook."

"Why?"

"Because it'll kill your mother if Emma's arrested."

"I've thought of that too," Mark said quietly.

"Should we stop investigating?"

"You don't mean that."

"No." She didn't. She still believed it important to uphold justice.

At Anne's door, he gathered her to him. "Mom'll be all right. She's tougher than she seems."

20

*B*oy-oh-boy-oh-boy," said Madeline flicking on the light.

Rudely awakened, Anne bolted up in bed. It was 2:00 A.M., hours after she and Mark had left his parents'. Eager to tell Madeline about the engagement, Anne had forced herself to stay awake for a while but had fallen asleep before Madeline returned. She groaned, flopped down, and pulled the sheet over her head.

"Oh, excuse me," said Madeline, "I forgot you were here." She flicked off the light.

The strange comment startled Anne and fully woke her. She sat and turned on the bedside lamp. "Where did you *think* I was?"

"Here, of course. I forgot because I'm frustrated."

"About what?"

"Rick."

"You mean because he refuses to be a tycoon?"

"No, but of course that still annoys me. What really gets me frustrated is he can't work up the nerve to kiss me. He holds my hand and gives me love-struck looks, but that's it."

"That's because you intimidate him."

Madeline scowled. "Then that does it. He's got to take assertiveness training. Since you brought it up, you speak to him," she ordered.

"No!" Anne said emphatically. "Rick has a quiet, reserved personality—let him be himself!"

118

In her frustration, Madeline yanked a blue silk night-gown from her drawer and pulled it over her head. "You are no—absolutely *no* help!"

Anne grinned at Madeline's dramatics, then waved her hand under the bedside lamp. Her diamond sparkled.

"What is *that*!" said Madeline, her eyes wide and stunned.

"It's from Mark. We're engaged."

"*Engaged!*" Madeline exclaimed, still shocked.

At times Anne had wondered if Madeline were completely over her feelings for Mark. She would never wonder that again. With a laugh of delight Madeline pulled Anne out of bed and hugged her. "I'm so happy for you," she said softly.

"I hoped you would be."

"You deserve the best," Madeline said.

The affectionate comments were a little out of character for Madeline, and she reached for her cigarettes, busily lighting one up. By the time she had arranged herself on her bed, she was her normal aggressive self. "I'll be the maid of honor, of course."

Anne smiled, at the moment loving her. "Of course."

Madeline added, "Green's my best color. I prefer a long dress."

"Whatever you'd like."

"Well, I don't want to look like an eighth grader at a dance."

"Of course not."

Though Anne had the next day off, Madeline didn't, and the thought made her frown at the bedside clock. "We'll finish planning my dress tomorrow," she said as she turned off the light.

———

Because of the enormous cost, air-conditioning the inn

was out of the question, so ceiling fans were used to cool the rooms. Usually they did an adequate job, but today the fans were no match for the afternoon sun, and most of the guests were steamed out of the inn.

Anne was heading for the beach, but before she reached the door, Weedy called her to the front desk. "I'm disappointed in you," he said in a grief-stricken voice. He raked his hands through his brown hair. "Why are you marrying him when you could have me!"

Anne grinned at his mock misery. "I didn't think of it."

"Reconsider!" he cried.

"No."

"Was I a close second?"

"Yes," Anne laughed and ran off.

At the beach, Anne laid out her towel but she didn't lie down. Rick was sunning on the raft, so she entered the warm water and swam toward him. When she was a few feet from him, he looked uncertainly at her, as if he thought he might know her but wasn't sure. *His contacts aren't in*, Anne thought, and she called out, "It's me, Anne."

He smiled and rose to pull her up onto the raft.

They lay on their stomachs with their heads propped on their hands. "It's hot," he said. Because Rick found conversation difficult, he usually began a conversation with comments on the weather.

"Very."

"It's ninety-two or more. I didn't catch the latest report."

"Ninety-three now." Actually, Anne liked talking about the weather; it was relaxing. Especially considering the wild pace of events these last two weeks.

"Really?—that hot?" Rick said. He smiled. "Congratulations. Madeline told me you're engaged. She said she'll be in the wedding."

"Right," Anne said, and told him about Madeline's green dress.

Rick's mouth formed a slight frown. "Don't you care for green?" Anne said.

"It's not that. It's that I wish I had Mark's nerve."

"What do you mean?"

"So I could propose to Madeline, of course."

Anne would rather he didn't. It would be awful for Rick to marry someone who loved his money more than him. Anne secretly hoped he would come to the conclusion that Madeline wasn't the woman for him.

"You hardly know her," Anne said.

"I loved her immediately," he said.

"How do you know she loves you?"

"She's always after me to improve. To me, that's love."

Anne sighed and sat up. "I'm not sure it is."

"I am," Rick said emphatically. He lifted his head up from his hands. His eyes shone bright with admiration for Madeline. "She's just about perfect."

"Nobody's just about perfect."

Rick didn't hear her. "What do you think's a good way to propose?"

Anne jumped up, thoroughly distraught. She had to stop him. She knew Rick was a Christian; she decided to appeal to his spirit. "Have you asked God if He wants you to marry Madeline?"

"Is that what you did before you got engaged?"

Rick had struck a nerve. Sure that her distress showed, she turned her head as she said, "No."

"Why didn't you?"

"Because I didn't, but that doesn't mean that you shouldn't."

"Maybe I will, but I don't know."

"Try," Anne said, and jumped into the water. She

couldn't talk anymore about prayer because she felt so heavy with guilt.

———————

When Anne came in from the beach later, she found Madeline stretched out on the bed, mopping the perspiration from her face. "I was absolutely mad to sign on at this dump," she said with a scowl, expressing her disdain. "Laborers and farmers are expected to perspire, actresses aren't!

Anne changed into shorts, curled up in the easy chair, and thought about Rick. When confronted with a decision, he swayed like a blade of grass between his alternatives; yet when he chose his course, he stuck to it. He had made up his mind to propose to Madeline and Anne doubted he'd change it. *I'd better take matters into my own hands*, she thought.

In light of Madeline's mood, this was a poor time to do it, but she was too worried about Rick to delay. "I just talked to Rick and he wants to propose," Anne said. It was a plus in Madeline's personality that she was direct and one could be direct with her.

Madeline dropped her handkerchief and shot from her bed. "Now?" she said loudly.

"No, not now, but sometime soon."

"I'll wear the white linen dress," Madeline said, not seeming to hear.

To keep Madeline from pulling out the dress, Anne quickly added, "Not now—don't change—please listen. He's not about to propose, he's just thinking about proposing—he's trying to get up his nerve."

Though Madeline stopped beside the dresser, she strained toward her closet.

"You can't marry him!" Anne said.

"Why not?" Madeline said with irritation.

"Because you'll hurt him. He'll be crushed when he finds out you're not as fond of him as of his money."

"Nonsense. I love him in my own way."

"That's not enough."

"It's more than enough. He dotes on me—nothing would make him happier than marrying me."

Madeline lay down again and fanned herself with *Vogue*. "I must find a way to steer him into a proposal," she said.

I was a fool to meddle in Madeline and Rick's relationship, Anne thought, appalled that matters were so out of hand. By all appearances, it was possible Madeline and Rick could be married before she was.

21

*T*wo hours before the engagement party, Tessie's two three-tiered cakes with hearts and roses were at one end of her dining room table, the punch bowl and cups at the other, and Tessie between them, pressing her hands against her cheeks, greatly distressed. "What'll we do—what'll we do?" she muttered.

Anne's father had just phoned with the news that a parishioner was undergoing emergency surgery, and he needed to be at the hospital with the family. He wouldn't be attending the party. Though Anne hated to admit it, she was relieved. His presence would have reminded her that he didn't really approve of her engagement. "We should go ahead with the party," Anne said.

"But we can't have the party without your father!"

Tessie had invited 150 guests, 50 more than she had promised Jim she would. Just yesterday when the telephone repairman worked on the line, he too had been invited. "He seemed so nice," Tessie explained to Jim and Anne. "Good grief!" was Jim's reply.

Anne assured her, "You can't cancel out now. It's too late to contact all those guests."

"Well—"

"Really," Anne said firmly.

Tessie gazed at her cakes. "They're all made."

"Right, so let's go ahead."

"Okay," Tessie said. The decision made, she brightened

and pushed Anne toward the door. "Run along and get dressed and I'll see you soon."

Anne left, and when she got to her room, she found Madeline already dressed in a slim green dress that exactly matched her eyes. Her black hair was caught up in a loose topknot. She looked stunning. To Anne's surprise, as much as Madeline had hinted and steered, Rick hadn't yet proposed. Anne assumed he had prayed and was reconsidering, though she was determined not to ask. She certainly wouldn't meddle again.

Anne questioned Madeline, "How come you're dressed so early?"

"I'm going to help you dress," Madeline said crisply, though her eyes were warm.

"How come?"

"Because you don't know how. You don't make the best of yourself."

Madeline plugged in a curling brush, and while it heated, she expertly applied Anne's makeup. She then curled Anne's hair just enough to give it body. While Anne waited patiently, Madeline chose a dress of her own and eased it over Anne's head. "It's not bad," said Madeline, studying the fitted white sundress.

But Madeline wasn't completely satisfied. She took an exquisite pearl necklace from her jewelry box and fastened it around Anne's neck. Now Madeline's face registered satisfaction. "You look lovely," she said softly.

The moment was special. Madeline might just as well have said, *I really love you, Anne.*

Anne blinked back tears. "Thanks for helping me."

"No problem."

When Mark called for Anne, she floated out the door, feeling beautiful and totally in love. But, oddly, as they walked down the corridor she felt a chill inside. Was she fearing that something would ruin their future? No, nothing possibly could.

Mark stopped her, pulled her into his arms, and whispered, "I must tell you again that you look absolutely gorgeous. I've never seen you so beautiful."

He lightly kissed her lips, then again. Though no one was around, Anne feared someone would be soon. Furthermore—and unaccountably—his affection disturbed her. Why? "The people," Anne said, "we should get to the party."

"Okay," he said, releasing her. "Very soon we'll be married—and alone."

The McGills' living room, dining room, study, and kitchen were jammed with guests, including the telephone repairman. Anne greeted him, not surprised he had come. People almost always accepted Tessie's invitations. The apartment was hot and stuffy, even though the windows were open and the ceiling fans were on full force. Tessie was in her element, dashing joyfully from guest to guest, perspiring heavily, and looking all too like a wet daffodil in her damp yellow dress.

After the cake and other refreshments had been served, Anne and Mark circulated; but somewhere in the crowd, Anne lost Mark and found herself face-to-face with Emma.

The party had been so nice, now this. Emma amusingly reminded Anne of a bullet in her charcoal suit, with a skirt that narrowed in at the knees. Her face was a scowl, which Anne partially returned. *Why pretend?* Anne thought. *She hates me and I'm not fond of her.*

"Hi," Anne blurted, stepping back, intending to walk casually away.

"Stay a minute, please," Emma demanded.

Emma sipped slowly from her punch cup, taking her time before speaking. "Seeing is believing."

"What do you mean?"

"Seeing this engagement party. Until tonight, I was sure Mark would come to his senses and call it off."

Anne seethed. She had no reply.

"Are you and Mark planning to live here?"

"No, in Reily."

"Good," she said, twitching her mouth into a smile.

Anne sensed what was coming.

"I'm not a fan of yours, you know . . . the farther *you* are from me, the better!" With that, Emma spun on her heels and left.

Anne glared at Emma's back, hating her own feeling of anger, and suspecting that Emma rather enjoyed it. She certainly had succeeded in dampening the party for Anne.

Rick suddenly appeared, looking businesslike in an expensive navy suit and tie. Madeline must have dressed him too! "You look awful," he said. Startled at the inadvertent meaning in his remark, Rick's face contracted. "I mean, you look very beautiful but you don't look happy."

"I'm not."

"Is it Miss McGill?"

"Yes."

"Don't pay any attention to her."

"I think she was born mean."

"No, she's unhappy," Rick said, blinking apologetically to show he disliked forcing his opinion.

"She makes me furious. She's ruined the party for me."

"Aren't we supposed to love everybody because we're Christians?"

"Yes, but not their actions."

"But we *are* supposed to love *them*."

"I'll try." She would, but not tonight—not when Miss McGill was the last person she cared to think about. She did feel better though; planning to make an effort to love Miss McGill in the future diluted Anne's present misery.

Rick scanned the room.

"Are you looking for Madeline?" Anne asked.

"Yes, I lost her someplace, and if I don't find her she'll be upset. She likes me to stay with her."

"What you said helped. About Miss McGill, I mean."

Rick grinned, then pushed off through the crowd after Madeline.

Anne and Emma didn't meet again, and when the last guest had left and Anne was at the door saying good-night to Tessie, she was able to say sincerely, "The party was wonderful."

"You don't think the punch was too spicy?"

"No," Mark said.

"It's Aunt Hazel's cousin's recipe, and that family tends to like things spicy."

"It was perfect," Anne said. She lovingly traced Mark's face with her eyes. "Everything's perfect."

22

The next morning, when Madeline's dresser drawer creaked open, Anne sat up in bed, rubbed her eyes, and yawned. "Forgive me," said Madeline, "but there's no way to open this broken-down thing without waking the entire floor."

Last week Jim McGill had fired Pam, and Tessie hired an efficient woman who had worked at the inn several years ago. Tessie now had several good replacement waitresses to draw on and she was able to give both Anne and Madeline the day off. Anne planned to go to church, and Madeline was going to Grand Rapids to meet Rick's parents at their country club—the most exclusive country club this side of Detroit, according to Madeline.

Madeline wore a striking houndstooth-check suit, a white silk blouse, and black heels. As she closed the dresser drawer, she said, "I couldn't look better. Rick's parents are bound to be impressed. When Rick sees their reaction, he's sure to propose."

Anne kept quiet.

"I can tell by your dim-eyed look that you still hate the idea of my marrying Rick."

You won't get me to answer that, Anne thought.

"I should think you'd be delighted. Wasn't I delighted when Mark took off after you and dropped me?"

The exaggeration shook a response from Anne. "No, you weren't. But you were nice about it," she conceded.

"That's the point. I was nice about Mark; you be nice about Rick."

Anne laughed. "You're impossible. The situations aren't the same and you know it."

Delighted to be thought impossible, Madeline smiled coyly as she dabbed behind her ears with her most costly perfume. She picked up her purse and left abruptly.

At a few minutes before eleven, Anne arrived at church and sat in the fifth pew on the right side of the aisle, where she usually sat.

Reverend Lindsey was in the first pew of the choir loft with his head bowed, his clerical robe hanging loosely from his wide shoulders. Because he disliked formal entrances, he always seated himself before the choir entered the chancel. The organ struck up the majestic "Crown Him with Many Crowns," the choir filed into the chancel, and the congregation stood. Anne stood with them, as she had hundreds of times. Behind her a woman trilled in a scratchy soprano, and Anne didn't have to turn to know it was the buxom Mrs. Hopple. Though Anne couldn't see her face, she knew by the little blue hat that Mrs. Maple stood in the second row. Mrs. Maple was seventy-three, and she had grown old in this church, wearing little hats with veils or flowers or ribbons.

Anne knew every person in the sanctuary; they were her family. Anne sang in her full alto voice. "Crown Him with Many Crowns" filled the sanctuary, and Anne felt a wonderful merging, a complete sense of being at home.

Then suddenly she felt strangely torn from the people, standing off where no one could touch her. She began crying softly. What had happened? Why was she suddenly feeling so alone and miserable?

Anne didn't hear her father's sermon. Her eyes were drawn to the stained-glass window she had always loved best, the one that depicted Jesus surrounded by the children.

She saw how the children loved Him and how He loved them, and she began to understand why she felt alone.

It wasn't the people she stood apart from, it was Christ himself.

She had taken one big step away the night she accepted Mark's ring, violating God's Word that a Christian should not marry a non-Christian. Other smaller steps had followed.

Every step was sin, every step broadened the distance between her and her Lord.

There was only one way back to God, and she'd have to take it.

Pain tugged at her heart and tears streamed down her face. She covered it with a tissue. Maybe she had always known she would come to this conclusion. Maybe that was why she had treasured every moment of her engagement, perhaps instinctively knowing she was living a fairytale, on an eleven-day trip away from God.

I love Mark, she thought. *But I love you more, Lord.*

When the benediction had been said, Anne stepped into the aisle, waiting with the rest of the congregation to greet Dr. Lindsey.

When she told him what she was going to do, she knew he would be pleased, not just because she had heeded his advice, but because she was listening to God.

She stood before her father now and he took her hand. Her face was white, her eyes red. "I'm calling off the engagement, Dad," she whispered.

He studied her face, and she knew he saw her grief and realized the cost to her. His eyes filled. "I love you, kitten."

"Forgive me for going against you like I did."

"I already have."

Mr. Lowe, a precise man who always ate his Sunday dinner at 12:30, impatiently cleared his throat, urging Anne on. Anne's father wrapped her in his arms. "Good-bye, kitten."

23

Why, today of all days, did Mark take a day off to go fishing on Lake Michigan with his friend Peter Flaxman? They were out on Peter's Boston Whaler, and they intended to fish until dusk. Anne slid off the pumps she had worn to church and sank into her easy chair. No, she decided, it was best he was fishing—best she didn't have to break the engagement just yet; she needed to think. She dreaded hurting him. She needed to find the best way of breaking the news to him.

Anne's stomach felt queasy, and she skipped both lunch and dinner. She was still in the easy chair when Madeline came back from Grand Rapids at 8:00 P.M. "How was your day?" Anne asked in a listless voice.

Madeline swooped over to the dresser, set down her purse, and with elaborate gestures began, "Lovely, absolutely marvelous. The club had Persian carpets, waiters in starched jackets, silver chandeliers. Money, Anne, that's what I saw. Money all over the place."

Her arms stretched up in a luxuriant arc. "Rick's mother wore a plum-colored Cadberry original—worth a mint. Even *I* have never bought a Cadberry."

If only it weren't so difficult to sound interested in the elegant Mrs. Hobert and her elaborate club. "Oh," Anne said as brightly as she could.

Madeline continued, "I absolutely loved the Hoberts and they loved me. I'm positive Rick was impressed with

how I fit in. Frankly, I believe he was on the verge of proposing."

Anne picked up a book, deciding it would be better to
pretend to read than to listen to a depressing account of how
Rick was about to propose. She had enough on her mind
without adding that.

But Madeline wouldn't let her get by with it. "Why are
you shutting me out?"

"I'm not."

"Don't give me that!"

Surely all she had to say was: I don't want to talk about
Rick. But Madeline's exclamation must have shocked her
system, because her emotions spilled over and she blurted,
"I've got to break up with Mark."

"Break up?" Madeline said in an astonished tone.
"Why?"

"I really shouldn't say, because I haven't told him yet."

"You can't start telling something and not finish it!"

Maybe all along she had really needed to tell Madeline,
for it relieved her some as she explained. To be sure Madeline fully understood, she shared with her 2 Corinthians
6:14–15 that talks about a believer having little in common
with an unbeliever. But predictably, Madeline was not understanding. As she hung her suit on its matching silk-
covered hanger, she shot Anne an irritated look.

"You're nuts!" Madeline said. "You're carrying your religion to an extreme. Nobody breaks off with the man she
loves because he's not a Christian!"

Madeline's voice escalated. "Don't be a fool! Don't tell
Mark what you've told me!"

Madeline's passion outstripped the occasion and Anne
said, "Why are you so upset?"

"Do you really want to know?"

"Yes."

"Your belief in God maddens me. There is no God. It's

crazy to throw away everything for nothing."

"Do you really believe that?"

"Absolutely."

"You're wrong."

"I doubt it."

"God tells everyone that He exists."

"How?"

"By what He's made—nature."

"Nature! I expected something more profound."

"It is profound."

Madeline wandered to the window, gazed out at the trees, and fell deep into thought. The evening sun laid a golden haze on her face and planed the sophisticated lines. She looked younger.

Finally Madeline said, "I've always wondered where trees came from."

"Then you've thought God might exist?"

"I've hoped sometimes," she gulped.

Madeline had hoped! "Madeline, you—"

"That's enough. I'm not used to talking about this kind of thing." Madeline was firm.

That was that. How Anne hated to leave it there.

———

It was after ten when Mark finally phoned Anne. He had hoped to be back earlier, but Peter had wanted to stop for coffee. Anne asked him to walk with her to Rosses' beach, where it would be private. She hoped he would feel less hurt there, because he loved the lake.

They sat in the sand, and the slice of moon, like a soft candle, weakly lighted Mark's face. *Oh, Mark,* she thought, *how can I possibly say what I've got to say?*

"Mark," Anne said, "I—" She began to cry.

"What's the matter?" Mark drew her into his arms. His embrace was so tender, so understanding, she began to give herself up to him, to lose her resolve.

Dear Lord, Anne thought, *give me the courage to speak.*

Anne drew away. "I can't marry you."

He looked stunned. "Why?"

"You're not a Christian."

"What on earth are you talking about?"

"I can't marry a non-Christian."

"We've been through all this. You said you weren't as fundamental as your father."

Oh, this was awful, worse than she had imagined it could be. "I was wrong."

His face changed, and he was angry—almost brutal in his speech.

"I won't let your twisted interpretation of Scripture wreck our lives!"

"It's God's will for me."

"*That* I doubt."

"I wouldn't do this to you if it weren't, Mark."

"Hardly. You follow any whim that hits you and then use God as an excuse."

Crushed, Anne dissolved in tears.

Mark softened then. When he spoke his voice was gentle. "Anne, please come to your senses. Don't throw away what we have."

Though she had promised not to broach the subject, she was compelled to voice her one small hope. "Could you believe?"

"No . . . not like you!"

He moved away, holding his head in his hands. Waves lapped the shore, the Rosses' house was shadowy behind them, the setting was the same as it had always been. But that was all that would ever be the same.

It was over. Then with God's strength, for she didn't possess the human strength to do it, she pulled the ring from her finger and placed it on Mark's knee. Quickly she rose and ran from him.

She didn't look back. *I'll never look back on tonight,* she thought. *Lord, help me forget tonight!*

When Anne dashed into the room, Madeline dropped her comb on the dresser and said, "Your face!" Anne's hand flew instinctively to her face.

"No, it's all right—I mean it's just so white—and wet." Madeline handed Anne a tissue.

Anne blew her nose. "You don't have to say a word," Madeline said kindly. "I know what happened without your explaining."

Madeline studied Anne. "I didn't think you'd go through with it."

Anne's voice was flat. "Well, I did."

"You gave up everything for your beliefs."

Silence.

"Well, I suppose I'm impressed. That takes guts."

The statement was startling enough to strike Anne's numb mind, but still she couldn't respond.

"Get changed and into bed," Madeline said.

When Anne had done so, Madeline said, "This is a lousy time to tell you, but I'd rather you heard it from me than from someone else. Rick finally proposed. He was a wreck, but he managed it."

It *was* a poor time, and Anne could only manage, "Oh."

"We'll be married after we both finish college."

Madeline folded Anne's spread and laid it at the end of the bed. "You'd better get to sleep," she said, and turned out the light.

In the middle of the night, Anne awoke. She wasn't sure of the time, but the room was dark, and Madeline was sound asleep. Because it was so long since she had felt such peace, Anne was particularly conscious of the strong feeling within her. It was the peace of God with her, not even a breath between her and Him.

24

The diamond ring on his knee reflected more of the thin light of the moon than Mark would have thought possible. He picked up the ring and dropped it in his shirt pocket. Anne was running along the path, but he lost sight of her at the bend, where her small frame merged with the trees.

He struggled against his desire to run after her.

He loved her.

A rawboned ache filled him.

How could she have broken the engagement? He thought the question of their religious differences had been settled. Had some fanatic from her Bible school gotten ahold of her and converted her? Had her father had a change of heart and taken her to task? Maybe because she was so young, she was fickle, incapable of sustaining her love for him, and therefore in the name of religion, called the engagement off. Again, maybe she had on her own given those troubling verses in Second Corinthians another thought.

He rose and paced the small, curved beach. One thing was certain: she was a religious fanatic and he'd been a fool to fall in love with her! His emotions raged from anger, to love, to grief. His eyes stung as if he might cry. But he wouldn't. He was controlled, a man who did not cry. He forced his character to override his love, his grief.

He'd make the best of this just as he'd made the best of all his circumstances. Hadn't he, with very little help from his parents, worked himself through college and law school;

set up a law practice, one that already was beginning to thrive? Wasn't he in complete control of his life? Of course.

He strode from the beach resolutely, his emotions in command.

When he came to the veranda, he casually greeted a guest, a middle-aged woman, short and plump, humped in a rocker. He didn't know her. "Did you just arrive?"

"Today."

She steadied the rocker and said, "Nice night." Her voice showed fatigue.

"Yes, very nice," Mark agreed.

He looked at her flabby body critically and surmised the kind of life she probably lived. When he caught a glimpse of a few candy bars in the satchel at her side, his impression was strengthened.

Whether he was right or wrong wasn't important. What was of importance to himself was that he was the observant lawyer again, completely in character.

———

Anne wasn't sure how Tessie found out about the broken engagement, but when she pulled Anne into the pantry the next morning and pushed her up against a row of tomato cans, it was clear she knew. Tessie's eyes were puffy, her apron wet with tears, and her hair unusually mussed.

Tessie pleaded with Anne to reconsider. "What's got into you, dear? You love my boy, I know it."

How in the world do I explain this? Anne thought, becoming panicky.

"Just tell me you don't love him," Tessie cried out. "Just tell me!"

"I can't."

"Then what . . . *what?*" Tessie sputtered, unable to verbalize the upsetting question.

"It's because I'm a Christian and Mark isn't."

"But Anne, Mark's a good Christian; he's one of the best Christian people I know."

In her own distress Anne had forgotten Tessie defined Christians as those who led good lives and non-Christians as those who didn't. "I know he's good, Tessie, but that doesn't make him a Christian. A Christian is a person who has given his life to Christ."

"He has!" Tessie exclaimed. "He was baptized when he was six weeks old!"

"That's not the same thing."

"Of course it's the same," Tessie said, grabbing Anne and squeezing her, as if to force some sense into her. "You must go to him. You must put this little fight aside. Take the day off. I'll call in Joyce to work in the dining room. Go to my boy and you'll get this whole thing straightened out. Now, *go!*"

Not able to stand another minute, Anne confessed: "I can't do that, Tessie. I'd do anything for you, but I can't do that."

At that moment, the milkman poked his head in, needing Tessie's order. Tessie ran her fingers through her hair, then gave Anne a pleading look and left.

Anne felt sick to her stomach. It was awful seeing Tessie so hurt. If only she hadn't gone through with the engagement in the first place, so many people wouldn't be grieving now.

That afternoon, however, Anne discovered that Emma was delighted the engagement was off. Dressed in her khaki bird-watching pants, she called Anne over to a corner of the parking lot and said, "I won't mince words. I'm quite pleased you won't be marrying Mark. You've shown some wisdom for a change."

In shock, Anne stepped back. *You cruel woman!* she thought.

Emma smiled, raised her binoculars, and trained them on a small brown bird on a branch of an Eastern White Pine.

The bird flew to another tree and Emma stalked after it, forgetting Anne.

Anne's thoughts sputtered after Emma.

But then she remembered the engagement party when she had promised herself she would try to love Miss McGill in the future. What an awful time to remember that! How could she love her at a time like this?

But something in her heart was telling her that now would be the best time. She had given up Mark for God; she could give up her dislike for Miss McGill as well.

Emma was in front of a spindly pine now, training her binoculars on a purple finch halfway up. *I love you, Miss McGill,* Anne thought.

It was simply a thought; she felt no love.

Then a series of thoughts came.

If my circumstances had been different . . .

If I had lived with a mean aunt . . .

If I weren't a Christian, I could be just like her. It's only by God's grace that I'm not.

Thank you, Lord, she thought, *for your mercy to me. Please be merciful to Miss McGill.*

Inexplicably, warm feelings for Emma came over her. She didn't feel love exactly, but she sensed that someday she would.

Anne slipped away and as she stepped on the veranda, she met Rick. His contacts had lint under them and were irritating his eyes. He rubbed them, which did nothing but turn his eyes red and watery. "Why not rinse them off?" Anne asked.

"I will," he said, but instead of taking care of it, he turned to her. "I'm sorry about you and Mark."

"It's okay."

"What happened?"

"I can't explain now. It hurts too much."

"Forgive me for asking," Rick said contritely.

"Sure. By the way, I hear you and Madeline are engaged. Congratulations." She had decided to just accept the engagement. She certainly hadn't managed her own love life well; who was she to advise him on his? Maybe he and Madeline would be happy. She hoped so.

He frowned. "Thanks, but after what happened to you, maybe we shouldn't talk about it."

"It's okay. It doesn't bother me."

"We'll have plenty of time to talk later. Madeline and I will be engaged for a few years."

Anne was relieved; she really didn't want to think about engagements right now.

But for two days, while all the staff and several of the guests expressed their surprise or disappointment or hope that Anne and Mark would reconsider, Anne was forced to think about nothing else. On each occasion she relived the awful moments at Rosses' beach. Fortunately on Wednesday it stormed all day, and the guests forgot the engagement and spoke of the ruined fishing, sunbathing, good times that they had paid for. Also on Wednesday, to Anne's great relief, Tessie stopped bursting into tears every time Anne walked into the kitchen. At one point, Tessie even took Anne to the pantry and said, "I've accepted it, and I still love you though I don't understand you!"

Wednesday afternoon Mark phoned Anne from his office and said that Earnest T. Blake would be stopping by that evening to collect John's things. His voice was crisp and businesslike, as if there had never been love between them. Had he already forgotten her? The thought hurt. *Stop it!* she thought. *What he thinks of you is no longer of any importance.* "Earnest is attending an insurance seminar in Muskegon, so it'll be late when he comes—about ten-thirty," Mark said. "Is that too late for you?"

"No—that's fine." Earnest had not sent John's letter and Anne asked, "Is Earnest bringing the letter tonight?"

"He hasn't found it yet, but he said he'd take one last look. He feels confident it will turn up."

John's things were still stored in his room, and Mark told Anne he would meet her there.

———————

At 10:30, when Anne arrived at John's room, Mark and Mr. Blake were already there. Mark looked terribly handsome. His skin was tanned, a result of the fishing trip Sunday, and his blue eyes were a striking contrast. When he introduced her to Earnest, his speech was as crisp as it had been on the phone. Anne was jittery; she hadn't yet dared be this close to Mark. At her request, Madeline had been serving his coffee at meals. Well, it was time she accustomed herself to being with him, to pouring his coffee. With deliberate, concentrated effort she managed to be calm.

Earnest was a magnified version of John—more burly, more florid, much louder. But, thankfully, Earnest was sober. He pumped Anne's hand heartily, commenting that he'd met all kinds of good people at the insurance convention. "I got a boost. Nothing's gonna stop old Earnest T. from becoming the number-one salesman in this great state of Michigan. The first thing tomorrow I'm calling fifty prospects."

He eyed Anne appraisingly. "Have you got a policy?"

"I'm on my father's."

"You need your own. Rates are good at your age."

"I'm not interested yet."

He handed her a card. "Keep me in mind when you are."

"He didn't find the letter," Mark told Anne.

"But I will," Earnest boomed. "Just give me a few more days. It's got to be in my bedroom. I've looked everywhere, but I do have quite a clutter in the bedroom—you know, papers and such. I'm a very busy man."

His eyes were certain, but Anne was dubious. "You're sure it's there?" she asked.

"Positive."

"It's really important we get that letter, Mr. Blake."

"He knows it's important." Mark sounded a bit edgy. "I told him that when I first contacted him about our investigation."

"I'd move heaven and earth for the sake of my brother," Earnest said. "I'll have that letter in my hand before I retire tonight. You can count on it."

Earnest opened the three boxes of John's possessions and emptied them onto the bed. He picked up a watch, a wallet, and a silver pen. "Send the rest to the best relief organization in the world—the Salvation Army," he said with exuberance.

"There's nothing else you want?" asked Mark.

He poked through the clothes again. "Nothing."

Earnest stuffed the items into his pocket and started for the door. "I gotta go. I need my sleep so I can sell tomorrow."

At the door he spoke again to Anne, "Don't forget, when you're ready for insurance, call old Earnest T."

Anne followed him out of the room, leaving Mark to pack up. She had made it so far, but she would fall apart if she were left alone with him.

When Anne finally crawled into bed she began thinking about the unsolved murder case. She sat up, leaned back on her pillows, and began to mull over with diligence the facts and possible solutions.

With Earnest pursuing his goal to be number one in insurance in Michigan, he'd have little time to search through his clutter for a letter. Furthermore, she really doubted he had much interest in solving John's case; if he had, he surely would have thoroughly searched his bedroom by now. Then, too, he might have tossed the letter out weeks ago. Even on the outside chance he came up with the letter, it could prove useless; Sergeant Marcum would most likely decide it didn't indicate Miss McGill intended to harm John. No, she couldn't base any hopes on that letter.

Being with Mark when others were around was difficult, but tolerable. Being alone with him was impossible.
She couldn't continue investigating with him; she would
simply have to go ahead on her own. Actually she had a su-
perior plan, one that would very likely produce the kind of
evidence that would cause Sergeant Marcum to reopen the
case. She trembled as she considered it. She would search
Miss McGill's room herself. It was the most likely spot to
find a letter, note, diary, journal—some written evidence of
intent to harm or motive to kill.

Getting into Miss McGill's room would be easy. Tessie
kept Emma's spare key in the left-hand drawer of her worktable. Though its location was certainly meant to be kept
secret, Tessie had inadvertently mentioned it was there.
Anne would get the key Thursday evening when the kitchen
was unoccupied. She'd go through the room Friday evening, immediately after she finished cleaning the dining
room. Emma would be at the weekly meeting of the Reily
Birdwatcher's Society. She was certain to be there; she had
been treasurer for five years and never missed a meeting.

If Anne found no evidence in Emma's room, then she
would allow Mark to finish the investigation in his own way.
He would probably wait awhile for the letter. If it didn't appear, he would present the other testimonies to Sergeant
Marcum and urge him to reopen the case on their basis.

Anne settled down and tried to sleep, but thoughts continued to nag her. Searching Miss McGill's room was probably illegal. But didn't she have to do all she could for justice? She was in it this far and felt she had to make this one
last effort. *What if Tessie notices the key is missing?* Well, she
had to take a chance, because she had to have the key
Thursday night. Friday evening was the only time she could
be sure Emma would not be in her room. Even at that, she
figured she'd have only about an hour.

She would just have to hope Tessie wouldn't notice the
key was gone.

25

*O*n Thursday afternoon, Hazel Green phoned Mark and asked him to stop by, stressing in her meek voice that the only reason she dared impose on his time was that she had a terrible problem. She couldn't reveal the problem over the phone; she must see him in person.

After work, when Mark rang Reverend Lindsey's doorbell, Hazel immediately answered the door. She was dressed neatly, but worry lines crumpled her face. She led him to the kitchen, refusing to share her problem until she had served him warm apple pie and coffee. Concerned for her, Mark had little appetite, but he ate the pie, knowing that nothing gave her more pleasure than pleasing him.

She perched her small frame nervously on the edge of her chair. "It's my son Georgie that's givin' me my troubles," she confided at last.

Because George hadn't helped Hazel at all when she had been in desperate need, Mark didn't think much of him. He couldn't conceal his contempt as he said, "What's he done now?"

"He tells me I gotta come live with him, and it don't make me happy to do that."

"I don't understand why that would be necessary."

"Georgie thinks it is," she shrugged.

"But it's not his right."

"He says his wife has gone to work at a grocery store and they need me to take care of the kids. He says it's my duty as a grandmother."

She tottered on her chair. "I guess I'm being selfish to want to stay here with Reverend Lindsey."

"Hardly," Mark said, angrily considering who the selfish one was. "Your grandchildren aren't your responsibility. You've got a right to lead your own life."

"Do you really think so, Mr. McGill?"

"I certainly do."

"Would you tell that to Georgie?"

"I would be glad to."

"Thank ya," she said smiling, relieved that it was as simple as that.

Mark left. He was glad to help Hazel, but more than that, he was grateful to have something to keep his mind off Anne. So far, he was managing fairly well, but last night when Anne left John's room, he had almost run after her to urge her to reconsider. But it was unlikely she would. He decided it had been a foolish thought, one he would guard against in the future.

———

While Mark was visiting Hazel, Rick was eating his dinner at the staff table in the kitchen. Madeline stood over him, glaring. She called to Anne.

"Tell him he *must* change his major," she fumed.

Anne sighed. Would Madeline ever stop nagging him?

Rick blinked and nervously pushed at his food, but he managed to say firmly, "I'm not going to, Madeline."

"You *must*!" Madeline said. "You must switch from chemistry to marketing to prepare yourself to take over your father's business. I will *not* allow you to be an insignificant chemist when you can become a high-ranking executive!"

"But I love chemistry," Rick moaned. "I love to work with paints. I want to develop new kinds of paint."

"Who are you marrying, a paint formula or me?"

Madeline spun her head toward Anne, her black hair flying. "*Talk* to him!"

"No," Anne said calmly. "How would you like him to ask you to give up your acting to become a teacher?"

"That's not the same." Madeline was calmer now. "Acting's a talent. Chemistry isn't."

"I guess it all depends on how you look at it."

"Maybe you're right, Madeline," said Rick, laying his fork down. "Maybe I *should* change majors."

"Of course!" Madeline returned, overwhelmed by his sudden change of heart.

"If you want an executive for a husband, you should have one."

"Rick, I'm so proud of you!" Madeline was ecstatic.

Anne groaned inwardly. It was so like Rick to give in to everyone. Especially to Madeline.

"It's settled then. I will change majors." Rick sounded convinced.

Since there was nothing more she could do or say, Anne left the room. She had been somewhat encouraged when she and Madeline had talked about God earlier in the week. But now it seemed Madeline was as determined, hard-driving, and aggressive as ever.

———

After dinner, Anne changed into jeans, waited until the kitchen was vacant, then took Emma's key from Tessie's drawer. It was a large key with a brass ball on it and it felt like a rock in her pocket. She was beginning to feel like a nervous wreck already, twenty-four hours before she would enter Emma's room. Would she be able to go through with it? Of course, she had to. If the case weren't reopened, she would always wonder if the evidence were up in Miss McGill's room.

Anne had forgotten to pick up her mail earlier and she

went to the front desk for it. Weedy was on duty and he gave her an affectionate smile. He looked ridiculous in a crew-neck sweater on a day like this. It was 73 degrees—sweater weather only for Weedy.

"What's up, barefoot?"

"I need my mail."

He handed it to her. "You need something else too."

"What's that, Weedy?"

He grinned. "To go out with someone again. How about a date?"

Anne doubted she would ever date again. But if she did, it wouldn't be with him. "I can't, Weedy. I'm real busy right now."

He frowned, then added with compassion in his voice, "Too soon after Mark?"

"Yes—really, that's it."

"Well—" He was stuck for words of comfort.

"See you later," Anne said, walking briskly away.

"Let me know when you're ready," he called after her.

Anne smiled. He was impossible!

———

Back in her room, Anne found Madeline in bed leafing through a well-thumbed issue of *Vogue*. Madeline tossed it on the floor. "I can't concentrate."

Surprised to find her in bed so early, Anne asked, "Why aren't you out with Rick?"

"We don't have to cling to each other," she said hotly. "We're quite capable of being separated once in a while."

"You act as if something's wrong."

Madeline adjusted the straps on her nightgown. Her hair fell forward, hiding her face. "Nothing's wrong. It's just that I despise mopers. Rick agreed to switch to marketing, and now he's moping over his decision."

Madeline seemed unusually distracted and continued

in a small voice. "I've gone too far with Rick. I've been telling myself I'm giving him creative career guidance, but it isn't that. I've been pushing him into a career he hates. I've broken his spirit."

When Madeline looked up, her expression was pensive. To Anne's surprise she began speaking about her father. Anne had wondered about Mr. Radcliff; except for the brief mention of him the night Anne met her, Madeline hadn't uttered his name. "He's rich and he's a hard drinker. When I was a child he was constantly occupied with either his investments or his liquor." She continued relating how she had frequently sought his attention, but never gained it. She particularly remembered an incident when she was seven. Her second-grade class cut black silhouettes of themselves from construction paper and pasted them on white poster board. Hers turned out especially nice, and hoping it would merit her father's admiration, she had shown it to him. He gave it no more than a glance and said briskly, "So that's what you do at your school." He turned away and dialed his stockbroker.

There was a faraway look in her eyes as Madeline whispered, "I was crushed. I don't think I ever recovered."

Anne wanted to reach out to her, but somehow it didn't seem the time.

"Right then I vowed I'd do great things to impress him," Madeline said. "Maybe that's why I want to be famous and have an important husband."

Madeline wrung her hands and moaned, "I shouldn't have pushed Rick so. It was wrong."

Anne remembered when Madeline had looked out at the trees, and they had spoken of God. "Do you believe in God, Madeline?"

"Yes—I think I might."

"He'll forgive you for hurting Rick if you ask Him."

"How could He?"

"Because His Son died for your sins."

"He couldn't forgive the things I've done."

"There isn't anything He can't forgive."

"I've been a snob. I've been vain." Madeline started to cry. "Anne, you just don't know how awful I've been."

"He knows, and it doesn't matter. He loves you far more than your own father could."

For a moment Madeline was still, almost attentive. Then her face took on its sophisticated look and her eyes narrowed with suspicion. She reached for a cigarette. "You're trying to convert me, and I won't have it!"

Madeline picked up her magazine and smoothed out the pages. "I'm quite tired," she said. "I'm turning in."

Anne felt like crying. She longed to pull Madeline back from her abrupt turn from God. *Lord*, she prayed, *Madeline was so close. Please don't let her wander off.*

———

The dull twang of the broken spring in the easy chair woke Anne before the alarm went off. It was 5:30 A.M. and the room was gray. Lake Crystal rustled like taffeta, rain drizzled down the window, and Madeline was sitting in the chair, her face a blank. "We need to talk," Madeline said. "I didn't sleep much."

Anne sat up and reached for the light. "Don't," Madeline said. "I prefer the darkness."

Had Madeline been crying?

"I can't stop thinking about God," she continued.

"Then He's trying to speak to you."

"About what?"

"About becoming a Christian."

"All right, explain it to me."

Anne explained God's plan of salvation in the simplest terms she could. If Madeline would repent of her sins and ask Christ to forgive her, He would. If she would give Christ her life, He would receive it; and He would be her Lord—forever.

"I'd like to do that," Madeline said simply.

Anne took Madeline's hand.

"What do I say?"

"Ask Jesus to forgive your sins."

Madeline bowed her head. "Forgive my sins. Forgive me for making Rick change his major. Forgive me for being so vain." Madeline's voice broke. "Please forgive my dad. I forgive him, too."

"Now ask Him to take over your life," Anne whispered.

"Please take my life."

Tears coursed down Madeline's cheeks. The power of God flooded her face, making her look more beautiful than ever.

Anne was crying softly.

"You're crying too." Madeline sounded surprised.

"Because I love you and I'm so happy."

"I love you too, Anne."

Madeline stood up and, glancing at the clock, said, "He should be up by now."

"Who?"

"Rick."

"Will you call him?"

"Yes, of course. I think I should, don't you?"

Madeline didn't wait but dialed immediately. Her voice was soft. "I'm sorry, Rick. I know now that I pushed you. You should be what *you* want to be, not what *I* want you to be."

Anne remembered 2 Corinthians 5:17, and she began to cry again. "Therefore, if anyone is in Christ, he is a new creation; the old has gone, the new has come!"

26

While Madeline and Anne worked the breakfast shift, the sky lowered and the rain settled in. With the exception of the elderly Mr. and Mrs. Compton, who seldom went out, the guests complained about the prospect of a dreary day in the confines of the lobby. "Poppycock," was Mrs. Compton's comment to Anne with regard to the complaints she had heard. "This is an average June—nothing like a few years ago when it rained twenty-five days out of thirty."

Anne's mind wasn't on the weather. She was preoccupied with the key hidden under her socks in the dresser, and the prospect of entering Emma's room tonight. "Oh," she said distractedly.

It was difficult to believe that in little over twelve hours, she would be finished with the investigation. Somehow the thought seemed ominous—but it shouldn't. She was simply nervous. Anyone would be.

After breakfast, Madeline sank in the easy chair and stated emphatically, "It isn't easy being a Christian!"

Anne smiled. What dramatics!

Madeline's lips were tightly pursed. "I'm serious! I realize now, you were right about Rick. I don't love him; I love his dad's company."

Madeline rose and paced nervously. "I've got to break

the engagement, Anne, but how *can* I? Rick will fall apart if
I do."

"He'll be okay."

"Not Rick. He has no will of his own. I want you to be
with him after I break it off, Anne."

"Okay—when?"

"Tonight."

*Not tonight! She had Emma's key; she was steeled for the
search. She couldn't possibly delay it.* "Couldn't you break
your engagement this afternoon?"

"I could, but why does it matter?"

"I'm busy tonight."

"Busy doing what?"

Should she tell Madeline? She had lost Mark as a confidant. Madeline could take his place. She'd stress to Madeline the importance of keeping her mission a secret. "I'll be
looking for a note in Miss McGill's—"

Anne broke off, deciding Madeline might think Anne's
action insane and urge her not to go. "I mean, I'm checking
on something for Miss McGill," Anne finished.

"Okay, I'll talk to Rick this afternoon."

Late that same morning, Mark arranged to stop by
George Green's at 7:00 P.M. Then because he had left several contracts he needed in his room, he drove to the inn for
them and stopped in the dining room for lunch.

The steady drone of the rain on the windowpane must
have lulled him, because as his thoughts moved from work
to Anne, he found himself gazing steadily at her while she
poured hot water for the Comptons' tea. He noticed her uniform was loose at the waist, as if she had lost a few pounds.
Her apron was tied unevenly, and the sash was frayed.
Though her cheeks were flushed, and her hair a bit mussed,
she looked as beautiful as ever to him. She was the same

Anne. Her spirit seemed to glow from her.

In two months she would no longer be working here. The thought shook him, and the feelings he had been restraining for several days broke through. He could no more control them than he could stop loving Anne.

He'd do what he had to do.

He waved Anne over to the table when he caught her eye. He said it bluntly. "I've decided to become a Christian."

Anne moved closer. "Really?" Her voice conveyed her surprise.

"Yes."

"Now?"

"Yes, the sooner the better—I suppose." His tone was matter-of-fact.

Anne's face didn't show the pleasure he had expected.

Mark continued, "I commit my life to Christ. Is that enough?"

Anne's fingers nervously traced the edge of the table. "It sounds like you've made a business deal."

"Well, in a sense that's what it is, isn't it?"

"You don't make deals with God!" Anne was incredulous. "You've got to repent of your sins first, Mark, then ask Christ to forgive you. Only then will you be ready to give Him your life."

Mark didn't understand and was becoming impatient. He was attempting to become a Christian for her, and she wouldn't accept it. She seemed able to draw only the narrowest of interpretations from Scripture. He was willing to follow Christ's example and lead an exemplary life, in his own way. But he wasn't ready to confess or repent. He would handle his sins—be responsible for his behavior. Why couldn't Anne do things his way for a change! "No—who's to say what sin is, anyway? Why does God—"

Anne's cheeks flashed red as she broke in. "It's God who defines sin. And He says you must repent of it to be forgiven. There's no other way!"

Crazy! He was furious with her. How could she be so narrow-minded!

Totally frustrated, she whirled around and ran to the kitchen, leaving the door swinging after her.

I don't get this business at all, he thought angrily.

I can't believe this is happening, Anne thought, slipping into the pantry where she could calm down in private. *Maybe Mark really wanted to become a Christian, and I've just blown it! Lord,* she thought, *if that's so, give me another chance.*

———

That afternoon, after Madeline had broken off her engagement with Rick, she dragged into the bedroom looking pale and lifeless. "Go talk to him, Anne," she whispered.

Anne found Rick rocking in a corner of the veranda. He was staring blankly into space as the rain splattered from the railing onto his slacks. "You should move your chair, Rick." Anne smiled.

He stood, moved the rocker mechanically, and sat again.

"Madeline told me."

"I suppose she also told you I didn't take it like a man." Tears welled up in his eyes.

With compassion, Anne said, "She didn't say that. She only asked me to talk to you."

"I cried, Anne. Can you believe it? I *cried*!"

"There's nothing wrong with that."

"According to my *father* there is."

"Well, *my* father thinks differently."

Rick's face contorted in pain. "Everything's gone wrong! I wish I were dead."

She felt sudden fear. Did he really wish to die—or was he simply expressing his despair?

"What do you mean?"

His eyes were wild. "I'm a fool!"

"You're not," she countered.

"Then why did Madeline leave me?"

"She was confused about what she wanted in a husband. Didn't she tell you?"

Rick rocked back and forth nervously. "I'm a failure—I couldn't possibly please her!"

Finally Anne entreated, "Rick, don't forget God! He can help you."

"Then why didn't He stop Madeline from breaking up with me?"

"Maybe Madeline isn't for you, Rick. Or maybe the timing is wrong."

"No, no, I can't accept that."

"Rick!" Anne pleaded.

"I prayed He'd give me Madeline."

"Then accept the fact that for now it may not be His will for you."

The rocker slowed and Rick was still. The wild look was gone. He bent his head and folded his hands on his lap. Quietly he whispered, "I accept it, Lord. Please help me to forgive and forget."

27

*E*mma would leave for her bird-watching society meeting immediately after dinner, and she had her briefcase containing her treasury reports under the table. Her outfit of a black skirt and gray blouse fit the mood the weather set. Anne brought Emma her pie, and her hand trembled as she set it down. The weight of the key in her pocket made it seem conspicuous, and she was almost afraid Emma would ask about it.

If only Miss McGill would forego the pie and leave so I could relax somewhat, Anne wished.

But of course Emma didn't leave until 6:40, the exact time she always left.

Just before eight, Anne untied her apron and laid it on a chair. She usually put it in the kitchen hamper, but she couldn't chance being detained. She needed every minute of the next hour to get into Emma's room, make her search, and get out.

Just as Anne reached the dining room archway, Tessie scurried after her. "Anne, dear, I've been waiting to talk to you all day!"

"Oh, I can't now, Tessie."

But she ignored Anne's comment. "The bird-watching society's decided to picket the insecticide firm, after all."

Anne tried to step away. "Good. I would be in favor of that."

Tessie secured her arm. "But, Anne, it's *awful.* Emma's

signed me up to picket! I can't bear to do that—I am a peace-loving person."

"I can't talk now, Tessie. Please."

"What should I do? I should support my daughter, but I just—"

Frantic now, Anne cut in, "I'll come see you later," and hurried away.

———

An hour before Anne headed for Emma's room, Mark entered the living room of George Green's tri-level. The extremely overweight man dropped with a thud into his recliner. He grunted as if the effort of letting Mark in was taking its toll. With the flick of a lever, a footrest snapped up his short legs. It was difficult to tell where George left off and the chair began.

He dug his hand into his shirt pocket, then hollered, "Mildred!"

Water ran in the kitchen; no one answered.

George shouted louder. "*Mildred*, get away from that sink and get in here!"

A tired-looking woman scurried in, nervously fingering her housedress. "Get my cigarettes," George demanded.

Mildred hurried away and came back with a package. George stuck a cigarette in his mouth. "Do you expect me to light it with my finger?"

Mildred obediently took a pack of matches from the end table beside George and lit his cigarette.

Mark was becoming increasingly angry and impatient as he watched the scene. He despised men that bullied women. It was all he could do to keep from punching the man.

"Are you the fellow who got Mother the job at Reverend Lindsey's?" Mildred finally asked.

"Yes—"

George interrupted, "Enough chatter. Get back to your dishes."

Clutching her bodice, Mildred scuttled from the room.

"Women!" George spat.

Mark's face reddened. He forced down his anger and explained that Hazel wished to stay on at Reverend Lindsey's.

"She can't," George said curtly. "The kids need their grandma. It ain't right they're left with a sitter."

It was difficult to believe that someone as insensitive as George could be concerned about what might be the best situation for his children. Mark began to notice the expensive gun collection in a corner cabinet, the large color TV, the stacks of magazines at George's side. It was more likely that he didn't want to spend the money on a sitter.

"Your mother's happy where she is. I think she should keep her job."

"She ain't," George said belligerently.

"That's where you're quite wrong."

"Nobody but *me* tells my mom what to do."

Mark's voice was firm. "Your mother is well able to make her own plans and decisions."

George's gray eyes began to flit nervously at this resistance to his plans. Mark noted his distress and decided the man was obviously a coward who got his ego boosts from bullying his timid wife and mother. Well, he knew how to handle that kind. Mark let his anger rise and stood to his feet, "If you cause your mother any problems—any problems at all—you'll have *me* to answer to."

"I don't answer to no one," George said, trying in vain to keep some command in his voice.

"We'll see." Mark was confident.

George fell quiet, then muttered, "Let the old woman have her way. She can stay in Timbuktu for all I care."

Mark left, but felt no satisfaction in George's assent.

Had he put a wall between Hazel and George? Would George forbid Hazel to visit her grandchildren? He was depressed when he stopped at his office to phone Hazel with the news.

Since Mark hadn't had dinner, he drove to *Richard's*, sat in a booth at the back and ordered the Friday special—chili with cheese, beans, and onions. He began to eat, but suddenly had no appetite and pushed aside his bowl. The day crushed in on him, from the conversation with Anne in the morning to the scene with George just an hour ago. *He must have upset Anne terribly*, he thought with pain. Of course, she couldn't have accepted the version of Christianity he had offered. If she had, she would have compromised herself. He even felt quite guilty about the way he handled the situation with George. Humbled, Mark thought, *I'm really not in much better shape than George.*

He remembered the scripture Reverend Lindsey had quoted to him: "For all have sinned and come short of the glory of God," and his comment: "There's a moment in every man's life when he finds himself measured against God's holiness."

Mark felt he was indeed being measured, and he came far short. He considered his attempt to escape repentance. Anne was right; there was no other way. He had to honestly admit he hadn't eliminated sin from his life—even though he had high standards. He was imperfect and would always be. He certainly couldn't applaud his behavior today—or on many other occasions. No, he was all too human.

He leaned his head in his hands and gave up his rigid control, tears filling his eyes. Dishes clattered as Richard cleared the booth behind him, but Mark was not aware; he was seeking the grace of God, seeking the Savior.

"Jesus, forgive me," he began.

"For hurting Anne—for bullying George, for thinking

I could handle my own sins. Please accept my life. I give it to you as it is."

His independent spirit dissolved, replaced by peace—a peace he hadn't known existed. He was awed and continued to bow his head. The incredible struggle within seemed to be over, and he could relax and rest.

The flooring creaked and Mark looked up. Richard was at his side, a coffeepot poised over his cup. "Anything wrong, fella?"

Mark smiled. "No. I'm fine."

Mark paid his check and left. He'd go to Anne and apologize for upsetting her this morning.

28

$\mathcal{M}$rs. Dobbin, a guest at the inn, was always running her fingers through her white, flyaway hair, wondering where this or that was. "Anne," she called as Anne hurried along the third-floor corridor, "have you seen my room key?" She was digging furiously in a purse the size of an overnight case. "I had it before dinner, but it's gone," she wailed. "Did you see it on my table?"

"No, I didn't," Anne said and kept on walking. She couldn't possibly stop.

"Wait!"

Anne paused. "I can't help you now, Mrs. Dobbin. Couldn't you get a spare key at the desk?"

"Couldn't you?" Mrs. Dobbin begged, tearing into her hair with both hands. "I wouldn't trouble you, but you're young and it would only take you a minute."

Surely if the key were on the table, Anne would have seen it. But even if it were there, she couldn't take the time to run down now. Still, she couldn't entirely abandon the frantic Mrs. Dobbin, "Let's take another look in your purse. It's probably in there."

"Oh, dear, it's so messy!"

"I don't mind."

Mrs. Dobbin handed the purse to Anne. She reached straight to the bottom, and to her surprise and relief immediately hit on the key.

With Mrs. Dobbin calling, "Thank you, you dear girl," Anne hurried on her way.

The delay heightened Anne's nervousness, and when she came to Emma's stairway her knees were weak. The stairwell hadn't been decorated for two or three decades. Worn carpeting patterned with eroded roses covered the stairs, and faded wallpaper of a bluebell and violet pattern barely covered the walls.

In contrast, Emma's doorknob was painted a bright yellow. *This must be Tessie's touch,* Anne thought. It made her chuckle to herself in spite of the tension she felt.

For a brief second, Anne considered bolting back down the stairs and forgetting the whole thing. But, she'd come too far to give up the search now.

She let herself in, quietly shutting the door behind her. This was the first time she had seen Emma's apartment, and she surveyed it quickly. The bedroom was off to the left of the small foyer, and the living room to the right. The living room was inviting with a fireplace in one end and a huge grandfather clock nearby. It read 8:15. She had plenty of time if she hurried. But she felt immobilized, still studying the room. Starched doilies perched on the arms of the heavy Victorian furniture. A score of stuffed birds with beady eyes hung on the walls. *Pull yourself together,* she thought. *Get going and do what you came to do.*

There was a desk beside the grandfather clock, which surely contained letters. But thinking it more likely Miss McGill would keep business letters in the desk and personal letters in the bedroom, Anne searched the bedroom closet, the nightstand, the dresser. Emma's things were neatly folded and carefully stacked by kind and color. But there were no letters, no photographs, no memorabilia of any kind.

Anne hurried to the desk. Under the desktop were four drawers and above was a closed cabinet with crudely carved doors. A closer look revealed branches with snakes twined around them. She glanced away at the grandfather clock. It was 8:40. She must hurry!

Anne opened the lid to the desk first. One of the pigeonholes contained a stack of letters bound with a rubber band. Anne's heart quickened as she took it and slid off the band. In her hand might be a letter from John! She leafed through them, but none were from or to John. How strange! It was 8:43. She had no more than ten minutes.

She was about to shut the lid and quickly look through the drawers when she noticed a thin drawer above the pigeonholes. Anne gasped as she opened it and found a small black diary that perfectly fit the drawer. She pushed the slide-button on the clasp. It was locked! Surely the diary contained the evidence she sought. Impulsively, she grabbed a poker from the fireplace tools, lay the diary on the floor, and slammed the poker against the clasp. The lock broke easily. She knelt on the floor and carefully scanned the pages. They were crammed with thick, black script—page after page of the details of Emma's life. It was as if her diary were the only true friend she had.

Anne quickly found the entry for June 3, the night of John's death, and read: "It was a cool evening, about 62 degrees. The moon was just past full, the sky very clear. John and I took a walk to the overlook. When we arrived, to my complete surprise, he said we were through! He said he had grown sick of my tirades. Tirades! I couldn't believe his accusation. Lectures, perhaps, but not tirades. He said he had far better times with Susan—that good-for-nothing waitress! I didn't think he'd actually die from the fall. I really didn't think of anything—I was so angry, I simply pushed him from the bluff. He screamed and landed with a thud. I doubt he felt much. I almost think I'd do it again. I'm better off without him."

Anne shuddered. How awful! How coldblooded and unemotional. Had she no feelings? Or was she afraid to feel what she'd done? Or was she . . .

Lost in her thoughts, Anne didn't hear the door open. The floor squeaked. Time froze, and the tick of the grandfather clock fractured the air. Anne clutched the diary. She raised her head slowly, knowing before she looked that it must be Miss McGill.

Unaware of anyone in her apartment, Miss McGill casually hung her gray purse on the coat tree and brushed a speck of something from the sleeve of her blouse.

Anne rose trembling, her mind a blank.

Then there was a loud gasp as Emma turned and saw Anne hovering beside the desk.

"What is the meaning of this? What are you doing in my apartment? Answer me!"

Anne managed to stammer, "I didn't expect you back yet."

Speaking had helped, and Anne's mind cleared. She had been caught, but maybe that wasn't so bad, after all. It would force Anne to confront Emma with her crime.

"Forgive me," Emma's voice dripped with sarcasm, "I forgot to inform you when I would return. If the occupant is out, then of course the caller is free to come in and poke through the occupant's possessions."

Anne took a resolute stance. "I always knew you were responsible for John's death. I came to find some evidence to prove it."

Again Emma was sarcastic. "How interesting. What made you so sure?"

"I added up lots of things."

"So you're a marvel at math." Emma's eyes bored into Anne's. "Does anyone know you're up here?"

"No," Anne said, and immediately regretted she hadn't said yes. She sensed danger, a strange foreboding within almost an evil presence. She had to escape and phone Sergeant Marcum.

Emma snatched the diary from Anne. "If you don't mind."

Anne reached to retrieve it, and in one fast move Emma struck down Anne's hand and threw her to the floor. Anne landed on her back, the carpet padding her fall. She was more stunned than hurt.

Emma laughed fiendishly. "You *are* in an unfortunate position, aren't you? It would've been far better for you if you hadn't become so fascinated with my affairs."

She means to kill me, Anne thought wildly. Intending to flee, Anne quickly sat up.

"Stay where you are," Emma barked, and stamped on Anne's fingers with the heel of her pump. "You're not going anywhere."

Pain tore through Anne's hand and she muffled a scream.

Emma was obviously pleased with the plight of her prisoner.

"That's good, my dear. We wouldn't want anyone to hear you." Emma snatched the poker, held the pointed head to Anne's throat, and forced her back to the floor. "Don't move!" Emma hissed.

"Why are you doing this?" Anne cried.

"Isn't that obvious, my dear? Isn't it clear that I'd rather your bad report be silenced?"

Emma pressed the poker into the hollow of Anne's throat. Anne gagged. "Please don't!"

29

At 8:40 P.M. Mark walked up to the front desk. Weedy pulled his turtleneck sweater to his chin and shuddered at the chilling rain that continued to fall. "It'll never clear up," Weedy moaned. "It might as well snow."

Mark laughed. "At the end of June?"

"It's been known to happen—especially when I'm around."

Mark laughed again, then said, "Have you seen Anne?" He was eager to find her and apologize, but he had checked her room and the dining room without result. Because she was forgiving by nature, he was certain she would forgive him for this morning, but he doubted she would believe he was a genuine Christian. Surely she would think he was presenting another imitation. He couldn't blame her if she did. It would take time to prove his Christianity. He only hoped with God's help that he could.

"I've got no idea. She doesn't tell me where she goes."

"Have you seen her at all since dinner?"

"Nope. Try Madeline."

Weedy pointed to the corner of the lobby where Madeline was talking to Mr. and Mrs. Compton. Recently, Mrs. Compton admitted that she couldn't hear and was wearing a hearing aid, but her husband was still holding off, insisting he had better ears than his wife. Mark went to them and asked Madeline if she had seen Anne.

"Not since dinner. She's—"

Mrs. Compton smiled and interrupted, "Have you and Anne patched up your quarrel?"

"Not exactly."

"But you must. If Mr. Compton and I hadn't settled our quarrels, we wouldn't have gotten married and had our two lovely daughters. I can't imagine what that would be like."

"What's that?" hollered Mr. Compton.

"I'll tell you later, dear," Mrs. Compton hollered back.

"Eh?"

"He's deaf," Mrs. Compton explained.

Mark smiled, and Madeline continued, "Anne's doing something for Miss McGill. Looking for a note—or checking out something."

"What note? Checking what?"

"I don't know. I would've asked, but I was upset about something at the time."

Mark considered the possibilities. Surely Emma hadn't sent Anne looking for a note, not at this hour, nor at any hour, considering how she despised Anne. Maybe Anne had been referring to their investigation. Evidently Anne had learned about a new piece of evidence—perhaps a letter or a note that Emma had sent someone. Or that Emma had tucked away somewhere?

If she were off looking someone up, he couldn't locate Anne, as he had no idea who that "someone" was. He considered the alternative. Where would Anne search for a note Emma had secreted?

There were only a few possibilities: Emma's office, her car, her room. Anne couldn't be searching the office, not with Weedy in full view. The car? Not likely. He had seen it in the lot—which meant Emma must be back from her bird-watching society meeting. Her room? *Oh no!* Mark thought. If Anne were in Emma's room when Emma arrived home—there was no time to waste! Mark whirled from the front desk and ran for the stairs.

"I've got an idea where she might be," Mark called. Weedy stood shaking his head.

———

Emma increased the pressure on the poker and Anne choked. Was Emma going to drive it in? *Oh, God, help me!* Anne prayed, almost fainting at the thought of such a death. "Please let me go," she coughed out.

"To the police? Do you think I'm mad?"

She is *mad*, Anne thought. Mad! She must escape. But how? Anne's eyes searched for a weapon. The only possibility was the floor lamp beside the desk. It was just inches from her hand. She thought she could reach back, grab the stand, and thrust it at Miss McGill, knocking her off balance. But she had to catch her by surprise. Emma was still poised with the poker, as if gathering courage to actually harm Anne.

At her first glance away, Anne reached back for the lamp, but Emma raised the poker and slammed it into Anne's wrist. She could hear the bone crack. Then in a panic, Emma struck Anne again across her knees. Anne's screams filled the room.

"Shut up, you idiot!" Emma was furious.

As Anne lay sobbing, the woman again held the poker at her throat, but seemingly without strength or courage to harm the girl further.

Anne bit her lip to force down her cries. *Oh, dear God,* she prayed, *help me!*

"Quite frankly, my dear, I'm delighted to have you under my control. You are a bit too nosey for your own good."

Emma's blouse had twisted from her skirt waist, beads of perspiration dripped from her face, her mascara and lipstick had smeared. She was grotesque. *There must be a way to escape!*

"Nobody crosses Emma McGill." She broke the brief silence. Anne tried to lift herself, but fell back. Her knees and wrist were so painful she was afraid to move. She closed her eyes, trying to imagine it was all a bad dream.

30

*I*n the split second before the door he had flung open cracked into the wall of the foyer, Mark took in the scene before him. Emma's hand was raised, clutching a poker. Anne was crumpled at Emma's feet, the hem of her uniform blood-stained. Her eyes were shut and her face was cold white. Was she dead? Horrified, he yelled, "Drop that!"

"Get out of here!" Emma yelled, and brandishing the poker, charged forward as if to attack him. Her eyes rolled crazily.

"Leave, you fool!" she screamed.

Then, suddenly, a look of horror crossed her face and she dropped the poker, narrowly missing her foot. Had she just realized she was about to attack her own brother?

"Sit down." Mark's voice was firm.

She drifted toward a chair, a blank look on her face. She seemed to have lost contact with herself.

Mark knelt beside Anne and gently lifted her shoulders and head to his lap. "Anne . . . Anne," he whispered, "it's me, Mark." He touched her closed eyelids with his lips. When they opened, it seemed he had waited far longer than a few moments. She was alive. *Thank God!* he thought.

"Are you all right?"

"I don't know," she whispered. "Where's Miss McGill?"

"Over there, in a chair."

"She . . . she—" Anne started to cry. Mark gently wiped

her tears, then examined the wrist she was holding. It seemed to be broken, as well as two fingers. Her knees were cut and bruised, but otherwise seemed to be okay. "You were out a few minutes ago. Did you faint?"

"I must have."

"Tell me just what happened."

He glanced at Emma, who appeared to be still in a state of shock. Anne explained why she had searched the room, what information the June 3 entry had revealed, and what had happened when Emma discovered her.

Mark was angry as he listened. She had behaved foolishly, impulsively. "What possessed you? You must know that what you did was illegal, besides being extremely risky."

Her eyes were stricken, and she stammered, "I wasn't sure."

"You should have consulted me."

"I couldn't."

He drove on, motivated by a desire to keep her from taking impulsive actions in the future. "But, why?"

She blushed and remained quiet.

He regretted he had embarrassed her. Then relief that she was alive overcame him, and he drew her into his arms. "Oh, Anne, I'm just so grateful you're alive."

Then, as if awakened to the seriousness of her injuries, Mark phoned the police and asked for an ambulance. Finally, he went to Emma and asked her to explain her actions, but she said nothing. What was in her mind? Was she recoiling from herself, from what she'd been about to do to Anne, from what she had done to John? Mark picked up the diary and opened it to June 3. What he read came as no great surprise to him, considering the meanness Emma had displayed toward him. *Still, causing John's death is a far jump from simple meanness.*

Within minutes, the ambulance, Sergeant Marcum, and Officer Harry Lester arrived. The attendants lifted

Anne onto a stretcher, and as they carried her toward the door, Mark spoke, "I'll call your father, Anne. I'll be at the hospital as soon as I can."

Whatever duties preceded this call had exhausted Sergeant Marcum. As he sat listening to Mark's report, his eyes seemed distant and his face literally sagged. After Mark had filled him in on all the details, he muttered, "This is the first time in forty years I've been wrong."

Mark didn't comment on the absurd statement, nor did he belabor the point that he believed Sergeant Marcum had handled the case incompetently. Accusation would accomplish nothing; cooperation would. For Anne's and his family's sake, he wanted the case settled as quickly and smoothly as possible.

Sergeant Marcum made a motion with his hand, a signal for Officer Lester to read Emma her rights. After she signed a waiver acknowledging that her rights had been explained, Sergeant Marcum asked, "Now, can you tell me what happened?"

Mark doubted she would speak. But with a flick of her head, she came out of her silence. "This is an unfortunate situation," she said primly. "Obviously I acted a bit hastily, but I did the human thing. I had no recourse. Anne broke into my room, went through my things, and broke the lock on my diary. She had no business in my apartment."

She tucked some loose hair into her shining bun and seemed satisfied with what she had said. Then suddenly she crumpled and wept. "Oh, my God, what have I done?"

Mark put his arms around her.

She grasped him and wept uncontrollably. "Don't let them take me away."

"You'd better go with them now. I'll come as soon as I see Anne."

At Mark's request, Sergeant Marcum didn't handcuff Emma. She allowed them to lead her away quietly.

————————

At the hospital Anne was given a shot for pain, her fractured wrist and fingers were reduced, and her knees were treated and bandaged. She was released, and her father took her home to her bed in the manse. The shot made her dizzy, and she could barely make out the faces of her dad, Mark, Madeline, and Hazel amid the roses on her wallpaper. Somebody smoothed the sheet and spoke of Tessie and Jim at the police station with Emma. Then someone gave her a sip of water, and that was all she remembered.

————————

When Anne awoke in the morning, her head was clear, but her mouth was dry, her lips felt puffy and cracked. She ran her tongue over them, but it didn't help. She fingered the cast on her hand. There was a dull ache through her whole body. Then she noticed that Tessie was huddled in a chair at the foot of the bed, looking terribly worried but strangely not noticing that she was awake. Anne smiled; it was good to see Tessie. "Can I have some water?" she said.

Tessie sprang up, kissed Anne, and handed her a glass of water, all in one smooth action. "Oh, Anne, I'd never have recovered if you had not survived this awful thing."

"But I'm okay."

Tessie stroked the lace of Anne's nightgown. "But you almost weren't."

This must be a terrible ordeal for Tessie, she thought. "Please don't worry. I'm fine, and . . . and I forgive Emma."

"Oh, Anne, how can you?"

"I just do."

"You're like an angel."

Anne smiled. Tessie seemed like the angel—so caring and loving.

Anne asked Tessie routinely how Emma was, and that

was all it took. Tessie collapsed in a heap at the edge of the bed and sobbed out that Emma was still at the station, where she had been charged with second-degree murder. Emma's lawyer said the charge would probably be lowered to manslaughter, but even at that he expected she would spend quite a few years in jail. "My poor little girl! Where did I go wrong?" Tessie cried.

Tessie's tender nature was stretched to the limit. Was there any way to comfort her? Would she ever get over this?

"It's not your fault," Anne said, but the words seemed feeble.

"It is, it is. I must have failed her somewhere."

"No, Tessie, it isn't your fault."

"Well, it does make me know you're right about something."

"What do you mean?"

"I mean about your Christianity."

Anne became excited at the turn in the conversation.

"I need it, Anne. I need what you've got."

Anne bolted up.

"Your father said that the doctor left orders for you to lie down, Anne," said Tessie, gently pushing her down.

"You were saying," Anne prompted, relaxing again.

"I can't go through this pain alone."

"Yes," Anne prompted again.

"I've decided to give my life to Christ, like you and Mark did."

"Like Mark did—what are you talking about?"

Tessie's hand flew to her mouth. "I've ruined it. Mark wanted to tell you himself. Forgive me, dear!" She rose and ran from the room. "And don't sit up," she called back.

"Wait, Tessie. Don't go. Tell me more!"

But Tessie was gone. Had she really meant that Mark had given his life to Christ? No—impossible, Anne reasoned. Tessie must have misunderstood Mark. Mark probably told Tessie he wanted to join a church, and Tessie had assumed he was a Christian. Though, why would he join a church? No, more likely that businesslike profession of faith he made yesterday convinced him he was a Christian and he had shared that fact with Tessie.

Then why, when she heard his irregular step in the hall outside her bedroom, did her heart start to hammer? Why was she so full of hope when in a moment she would be let down? He, of all people, wasn't a Christian. It couldn't be true.

Mark entered the room and sat on the end of the bed. Anne reached to brush her hair from her forehead.

"Leave it," he said. "I like it messed up."

She dropped her hand.

"How are you?" he asked.

"Pretty good."

"Thank God."

"And you. If it weren't for you—" She broke off with a shudder.

He saw the pain in her eyes and changed the subject.

"You remember our conversation about Christianity in the dining room?" he asked.

"Yes."

"I behaved badly."

"That's okay. Forget it. It's over and done."

"Something happened before I found you in Emma's room."

"You mean you had a feeling I was in trouble?"

"No—hear me out."

"But how did you know to come?"

"I put together a few things Madeline said. Anne, enough questions, I'm trying to tell you something important." He caught her uninjured hand in his, and though she struggled to free it, he clasped it tightly.

He told her what had happened at *Richard's*. She des-

perately wanted to believe him, but it was so possible he had
made another false commitment to Christ. Did he really understand? Her breathless voice revealed her hope as she
said, "Are you *really* a Christian?"

"Really, Anne. I really am this time."

He turned her face to his. "Look closely at me."

She studied his eyes and it seemed she saw a gentle light
in them, but that could be his love for her.

"Jesus Christ *is* my Lord," he said.

She had never heard him speak so tenderly, yet so truly.
She believed him now and she wept.

He took her gently in his arms and kissed the tears from
her cheeks.

Joy flooded Anne's heart. Finally—at last she could really love him! Forgetting her fractured wrist, she put her
arms around his neck and laid her head on his shoulder
where it belonged.

SPRINGSONG ❧ BOOKS

Andrea

Anne

Carrie

Colleen

Cynthia

Gillian

Jenny

Joanna

Kara

Kathy

Leslie

Lisa

Melissa

Michelle

Paige

Sara

Sherri

Tiffany

Anne

Muriel Canfield Kanoza

BETHANY HOUSE PUBLISHERS
MINNEAPOLIS, MINNESOTA 55438

Anne
Muriel Canfield Kanoza

Scripture quotation is from the *Good News Bible,* the
Bible in Today's English Version. Copyright © American
Bible Society, 1976.

Library of Congress Catalog Card Number 83–73597

ISBN 1–55661–584–1
SpringSong edition published 1994

Published by Bethany House Publishers
A Ministry of Bethany Fellowship, Inc.
11300 Hampshire Avenue South
Minneapolis, Minnesota 55438

Printed in the United States of America